Tale of the Jordn

Eric Hua

Published by Eric Hua, 2025.

TALE OF THE JORDN

First edition. March 16, 2025.

Copyright © 2025 Eric Hua.

ISBN: 978-1738040797

Written by Eric Hua.

Table of Contents

This book is dedicated to my friend Caleb and his family!

Title Page Illustrated by: Chelsea Wang

Chapter 1: Store Clerk

The realm of Jerusaleth, once a prospering kingdom, has since declined due to years of famine. Although big cities managed to survive, many villages and towns deteriorated. One example was Mahlon, which resembled a barren wasteland more than a town. The population had decreased by eighty percent, and many stores were abandoned.

It is here, where this story begins.

Entering a small shop in Mahlon, was a teenage man. He was calm as he walked in wearing a brown robe and holding a staff. He approached the clerk and ordered a couple of sacks of rice. After receiving the order, the clerk went to grab the two bags before returning to the counter.

"Not from around here are you?"

"How did you know?"

"Small town. I know all the locals here."

"Must make it tough for business."

"It's not so bad. The famine is what's really driving everything down."

"So why haven't you left?"

"To where? Anywhere you go, there the famine will be there also."

"Fair point. Nice talking to you."

"Hey. What's your name?"

"Its Shepherd." He handed the clerk some copper coins. It was enough to pay for the rice plus a bit extra.

"You are a good person Shepherd. Take care!"

With a smile on his face, Shepherd was about to grab the sacks of rice but someone kicked down the entrance. They both turned around and saw three men in armour with a sword sheathed on their hips entering the store.

The three men walked towards the clerk and as the leader approached Shepherd, he purposely bumped into him, forcing one of the bags of rice to drop. Once the lead guard was at the counter, he slammed it and spoke with the clerk.

"Well if it isn't my favourite store clerk in the city!"

"If I'm your favourite, why can't you even remember my name?"

The two guards near the door let out a small laugh as they thought the clerk's remark was quite clever. However, they received a deadly glare from their leader and immediately returned to standing in formation.

"You know why I'm here." He stuck out his hand. "Time to pay up the monthly protection fee."

The clerk pulled out a small stash and opened it. It contained a few copper coins but not enough to please the commander.

"What is this?! This isn't even enough to cover half!"

"It's all I have."

The guard put his arms around the clerk. "Listen, I completely understand that we are all in difficult times. However, if you don't pay the full amount, I can't protect you from unforeseeable accidents." He looked to his two guards and gave them the signal. Both of them began to knock things down around the store.

"No, please stop!" The clerk begged but the commander watched as his two lackeys continued their destructive ways.

However, the commander felt a small tap on his shoulder. "Huh? Oh, you are that kid from earlier. What do you want?"

"Stop."

"What? Speak up!"

"He asked you to stop. So stop."

"Tch, you got some nerve kid. I'm going to teach you some manners!"

As the captain was reaching out his hand, Shepherd reacted by moving away and then hit his heel with the staff, causing the guard to fall. The leader of the guards landed on his bum, and his two followers couldn't help but laugh.

Filled with anger because of the embarrassment, he drew out his sword and began to attack Shepherd. He swung his blade thinking there was no way the teenager would stand a chance but to his dismay, Shepherd avoided the blade with ease.

The clerk and the two clerks were amazed. "Lucky dodge." He then followed up with a few more swings but none connected. Sweat began to flow down his head as he was growing fatigued. He gathered all his strength for one more attack but Shepherd again rolled under the attack and this time, he tripped him with his staff.

Shepherd walked over to his opponent who was lying on the ground. He was willing to give his enemy a chance to leave, but the commander resorted to dirty tactics. He grabbed some of the smashed debris on the ground and threw it at Shepherd.

Some of it made contact with Shepherd's face, allowing his opponent to kick him in the gut. He then ordered his two lackeys to hold the boy down. With Shepherd restrained, the leader was about to teach the teenager a lesson. The clerk jumped onto the commander to save Shepherd but his efforts were in vain as he was thrown and slammed against the wall.

"You old fool. Guess I will have to teach you a lesson as well."

The commander unleashed his anger on the clerk and it was difficult for Shepherd and even the two guards to watch. They knew what their leader was doing was outrageous but they didn't have the guts to stand up to him.

The clerk had bruises all over his body, including his face, but the commander would not let up. The guards couldn't bear to look anymore so they turned a blind eye. With their attention diverted,

Shepherd felt their grip loosen, so he mustered up all his energy and knocked them both aside.

He looked to see the clerk barely conscious and his life in potential danger. Shepherd looked around and out of desperation, he pulled the sword from one of the guard's belts and threw it at the commander.

As the commander was about to deliver a punch to the clerk's face, he felt a blade pierce his chest. Slowly, he fell to his knees and turned his head over to see Shepherd, who couldn't believe what he had done.

With the commander's demise and his two followers still in a daze, Shepherd was confused about his next course of action. Immediately, the clerk grabbed the two bags of rice and gave it to Shepherd.

"Run!"

"But what about..." As Shepherd was speaking, the other two guards were starting to move.

"There is no time! Go now before they see you!"

Shepherd thanked the clerk and ran out of the store with haste. By the time he left the town, the two guards had gathered themselves. They saw the body of their commander lying on the ground and had mixed emotions. They too were not very fond of his presence. However, regardless of their feelings, a crime had been committed and they would have to return to their kingdom and report what had happened to their superiors.

Chapter 2: Uncle Joash

In the dark outskirts of the realm, lies an unsettling lair where the most sinister beings gather. The air was dense and the atmosphere was filled with dread. This was a place where very few mortals would dare tread.

Inside was an ominous being who sat meditating until the arrival of a couple of ravens appeared to bring him news.

"Intriguing, so the boy is still alive. My master would not be pleased."

He motioned for his ravens to leave and as he began to stand up, a woman in dark cloth armour stood with a mask that covered her face. She bowed in respect to the malevolent being.

"I have a mission for you."

She understood her orders and disappeared from the lair.

Near Mahlon, there was a small farm that had seen better days. It had been another difficult season as many of the crops could not survive that harsh climate. Despite the hardship, the lone farmer was found tilting the soil. He was wiping the sweat off his forehead when he heard someone quickly approaching the farm.

"Shepherd! You have returned!"

"Uncle Joash. There...something I ... tell... you...." He was so short of breath from all that running that he couldn't form full sentences.

"Breathe my boy breathe!" Shepherd took his time to recompose himself before speaking again.

"Uncle Joash, there is something I need to tell you! In the town I just visited I..." Before he could finish, his uncle threw him a tiller.

"Work and talk! It's more efficient that way!"

While Joash was hard at work on the field, Shepherd began thinking about how to bring up what happened in the town. He was afraid of how his uncle would react.

Would his uncle help him? Would he be horrified that he harmed another human? Would he be exiled from the farm? These were some of the thoughts going through his mind, and as he continued mulling about the subject, his negative thoughts grew stronger.

Noticing that his nephew was not putting in his full effort, Joash paused. "Hm? Wasn't there something you wanted to tell me?"

"Oh, it's nothing. We can talk about it later."

Joash could sense something was bothering him but he didn't want to pester his nephew. They worked until the sun was nearly set and then headed inside as they were both starving and hadn't eaten since lunch.

Dinner was nothing fancy as they simply cooked some of the rice that Shepherd brought back. The only thing added was a simple sauce, as food had to be rationed due to the ongoing famine. While they were eating, Joash noticed Shepherd eating slower than usual.

"So, what is it that you want to talk to me about? It seems to be bothering you quite a bit."

"I..." As Shepherd began to speak, he got flashbacks of what happened in Mahlon. He remembered the vivid details of the commander and clerk. His mind then showed him instances of his uncle being gravely disappointed and ostracizing him from the farm.

"I was wondering if you wanted me to take the sheep out tomorrow."

"Oh, that would be great."

"Okay, I will do that."

His uncle knew he was hiding something but instead of prying, he decided to take a different approach. "Hey Shepherd, just letting you know, you can tell me about it whenever you are ready."

"I know Uncle Joash. Thank you."

After they finished their dinner Shepherd helped clean up, before getting ready for bed. Although he struggled to fall asleep with all those thoughts going through his mind, his body was physically exerted and he would eventually fall into a heavy slumber.

During the night, in a city away from the farmlands, a woman concealed her identity with a dark cowl over her head. She walked through the city alleys, hoping no one would detect her presence. When she arrived at the end of the alley, there was a large wooden door that was locked. She approached the door and knocked. Although the door remained closed, the viewer opened and a voice could be heard.

"We are closed for business. Come back in the morning and you can buy a vase then."

"I'm not here to purchase a vase."

"Oh, are you lost then?"

"No, I hear this is where I go to see the toughest fighters in the city battle."

"I have no idea what you are talking about. Go home lady!"

Realizing her current methods weren't working, she switched her approach. This time, she pulled out a pouch that was filled with gold coins. "Do you know what I'm talking about now?"

The door view closed, but she could hear the door unlocking and slowly opening. The man placed his hand out and the woman threw the pouch at him. He inspected the contents to make sure they weren't counterfeit.

"Right this way." The woman entered and followed the man.

Chapter 3: Underground Arena

In the beautiful city of Horizon, a group of soldiers returned to the castle with news to report. They headed to the throne room where they were expecting to meet with the queen. Upon entering, there was someone standing near the throne with her back turned. The commander of the squad stepped up and bowed thinking it was the queen.

"Your majesty, we have urgent news to report."

The woman turned around but to the dismay of the commander, it was not the queen. "This better be important."

"Lady Athaliah, I was not expecting you. Where is Queen..." He was cut off.

"The queen is currently unable to see anyone."

"Is her majesty unwell?"

"The Queen asked me to keep that information to myself, but rest assured commander, she is fine. Until then, I have been appointed to take care of any business for the queen until she returns to her duty."

"Oh I see. My apologies Lady Athaliah, I was not told about this change."

"Tch, and you call yourself a commander? I'll overlook your failure this time. Now tell me, what is it that you wish to report?"

"Well, one of our commanders has met an unfortunate end."

"That's it? You came all this way to tell me that?"

"But, my lady, he was murdered by a teenage boy from the farmland."

"You are telling me a high ranking commander was defeated by a farm boy? How disgraceful."

"How should we proceed?"

"We don't have time to be worried about some lowly no name farmer boy." She was ready to leave the room until the commander spoke up quickly.

"But we know his name. I believe one of the guards who witnessed the event called him, Shepherd."

Lady Athaliah suddenly stopped. "What did you say?"

"Uh, Shepherd. I believe they said his name was Shepherd. Is something wrong Lady Athaliah?"

"No no everything is fine. But I have given the current matter some reconsideration. Send some of your troops and arrest this boy for his crimes."

"Yes my lady." He was about to leave but she had one last request.

"Oh commander." He waited for her to finish. "Bring him back to me directly."

Hidden from the daylight of society, was a place where only the strong and desperate would linger. Here lies the underground arena where scheduled fights occurred that were forbidden to the eyes of the royal city.

In one of the cells was a man with long hair. He closed his eyes as he was mentally preparing for his next fight. Once his mind was cleared of all distractions, he put dark-coloured markings on his cheeks and then wore his helm.

The battle was about to take place in a caged arena where two combatants had to fight until the very end. The stands were at about thirty percent capacity as only people with connections could attend. Anymore it could draw attention from the royal city, thus shutting down the entire event.

The hooded woman, who had been guided into the arena was trying to locate a vacant spot to sit. She had to pass some questionable characters to get to her desired seat. She wanted a good view of the fight, with a small crowd around her, and ease of access to a nearby exit.

Once she found her seat, the event was about to begin. Entering into the cage were two combatants. On one side stood the six-foot man with tattoos on his arm and a huge scar across his face so he wore a helm to cover it. Upon his entrance, he lifted his hands and the small audience that was in the arena erupted by shouting his name. "CALEB!"

The woman rolled her eyes. She thought he was the stereotypical meathead showing off his muscles, until she saw the opposing contestant.

The combatant was a hulking giant standing at nine feet tall. He had a massive javelin in his hand with a little man on his shoulder. His steps were heavy and almost enough to shake the ground. When he made it to the entrance of the cage, the little man wished the giant good luck before sliding down to safety.

The giant's entrance would have struck most warriors with fear in their minds but Caleb was not deterred. He stood strong and confident as the giant began his taunting.

"Little man thinks he can beat the Great Golly?"

"I don't think so. I know so!"

"Little man has to speak up. Golly can't hear you from down there."

Caleb had enough talking so he charged towards his enemy holding a Gladius in his hand. Most people would be frightened by Golly's size but Caleb saw it as his advantage. There was no way he could miss such a target. He began yelling a loud warcry as he aimed for an unarmoured part of the giant, his thigh.

However, Golly drove his javelin where Caleb was running, forcing the warrior to roll to safety. Caleb was surprised as he wasn't expecting his foe to have such quick reflexes. He knew he needed a new strategy but as he was recovering from the last attack, Golly pulled his spear from the ground, breaking apart some of the cement. He then kicked some of the debris, which hit Caleb in the gut.

After getting winded, Caleb took an elbow swing from the giant. He was sent hard against the cage. Golly made his way to the enemy and picked him up by the leg, hanging him upside down.

The woman in the hood covered her eyes as she couldn't bear to watch. Like everyone in the audience, she thought the battle was over.

"Haha, puny man all talk and no game."

The giant was about to strike the unconscious warrior but suddenly, Caleb opened his eyes and threw a sica on his sash. It struck the giant on the left side of his face, forcing Golly to let go. As Caleb was falling, he pulled a rope from his sash, looping it around the javelin Golly was holding. Because the giant didn't want to lose his weapon, he pulled back which allowed Caleb to have a lighter landing on his feet.

"Little man got lucky."

"Luck had nothing to do with it. I got you figured out."

"Liar!"

"Let's find out! Swing your weapon at me!"

The woman thought Caleb was insane, but after seeing how he escaped from his predicament earlier, she realized her initial assessment of him was wrong. She grew intrigued and wondered what trick he had up his sleeves.

As she continued watching, she witnessed the giant slam his javelin, damaging the floor. Caleb dodged the attack and then threw the rubble against the cage bars. It was creating a clanking noise throughout the arena. The audience was confused as to what Caleb was trying to accomplish but the woman noticed the giant wasn't moving.

Seeing his opponent confused, Caleb slashed one of the giant's thighs with his sword. The audience grew excited and the woman was slightly impressed. The crowd was chanting for the fighters to continue but a bell sounded that caught everyone's attention. Immediately, the crowd left their seats and made their way to the hidden exits.

Meanwhile, Caleb and Golly stared each other down before the little man came in to assist the giant. Seeing no reason to stay, Caleb left the arena feeling robbed of a victory.

Shortly after, a man guided a group of guards down to the arena. Their orders were to locate someone and there was a lead that their target had snuck into this area. When they arrived to the arena, they found the place empty without a trace of a single person.

"As you can see, this place is empty and hasn't been used in a while."

Although the lower-ranking guards were fooled, the commander of this group was not. He could see visible signs that other people had been there. However, knowing this place was not his domain, he felt it would be too risky to search the area. He gave the guide a mean look, before leaving with his guards.

Chapter 4: Journey Begins

On a beautiful sunny day in the plains, Shepherd took the sheep and allowed them to graze around. While the flock were enjoying their time, Shepherd was lost in his thoughts. He still couldn't shake his mind over what happened in Mahlon. The events kept replaying in his mind and he still wondered how he would bring the topic up to Uncle Joash.

He looked down on the ground, holding his head in defeat. He would have stayed in that position longer but could sense something was staring at him. Slowly he raised his head to see something staring back at him.

"Oh, it's just you."

"Baaaaaaa." Replied a sheep with black wool.

"Leave me alone, go frolic with the rest of your kind."

"Baaaa!" It headbutted him on the arm.

That was when Shepherd realized how insensitive he was. He momentarily forgot that this sheep was probably outcasted from its other members.

"I'm sorry, Ramsey. I didn't mean what I said. I just have a lot on my mind. Ugh, you won't understand."

"Baaaahh?"

"I did something horrible and need to tell Uncle Joash because I know he can help."

"Baaahhh!"

"But what if he yells at me or worse, casts me out? UGH! I DON'T KNOW WHAT TO DO!"

Again he had his head down but the sheep nudged him on his shoulder. Shepherd looked up as the sheep continued making noises, trying to communicate a message to him.

"You think I should tell him, don't you?"

"Baaah Baah!"

"Sigh... Fine. But if anything bad happens I'm blaming you!"

"Baaaahhh..."

Shepherd stood up and got ready to gather the rest of the herd. However, after taking a couple of steps forward, he stopped and so did the black sheep that was following him.

"Oh, thanks for listening to me ramble." The sheep smiled.

Shepherd felt a bit of relief but that wouldn't last as he sensed danger was lurking nearby. He looked around to see the shadow of a wolf hiding in the trees. Although he only saw the one, he knew that they hunted in packs.

He quickly whistled for his sheep to rally to him. From there, he made sure they stayed close together and moved as a whole unit.

The wolves that were hidden from their sight stalked their prey looking for any stragglers. However, Shepherd kept maneuvering around his flock, making sure he covered the weak point at every turn. He knew they only needed to make it a few more meters before the wolves would give up on their pursuit.

All was going well until he noticed that Ramsey was falling behind. He slowed down a bit to find that one of its legs was injured. There was no time to stop and assess with the wolves in proximity. He couldn't risk putting the entire herd in danger but he wasn't willing to leave the one sheep behind.

Shepherd looked around and saw the wolves beginning to leave their cover. They could sense the weakest link in the herd and they were ready to pounce on the opportunity. Sensing the hunters were drawing near, Shepherd picked up the injured sheep and continued moving. It caused the entire herd to slow down but their formation was solidified and the wolves hesitated to attack.

The predators surveyed the situation for a moment longer and when they realized that the herd would not separate, they turned away and gave up on their pursuit.

When he was certain his flock was safe, Shepherd let down his guard and breathed a huge sigh of relief. "Phew, that was a close one."

Ramsey walked up to his protector and licked him in the face. "Haha alright I get it, no need to thank me. It's what I'm supposed to do." He returned his attention to the herd and began leading them the rest of the way back home.

Home wasn't much further as Shepherd could see the house in the distance with the sun about to set. He couldn't wait to return home after a long day but he also had to confront his uncle. The more he kept putting it off, the more likely he would never talk about it.

He was mentally preparing himself but as he arrived near the entrance, he saw a couple of horses that weren't familiar to him. When he got a closer look, he saw an emblem on their saddle and recognized it from the guards in the town.

"Uncle Joash!"

Immediately, Shepherd ran towards the house where the door had been broken down. He searched through the place that had been ransacked, but there was no sign of his uncle. There was only one room left in the entire house and Shepherd gripped his staff tightly as he went for the door.

He busted the door open and swung his weapon ready to fight but when he got inside, he found four guards lying on the ground unconscious. Slowly, he moved towards the guards to find that they were still breathing.

"What happened here?" He was confused but he heard a voice that he did not recognize.

"You sure took your sweet time getting here."

He reacted aggressively by pointing his staff at the stranger. Shepherd could not see the man's face as it was covered by a hood, which gave him more reason to be vigilant.

"Who are you and what are you doing here?"

"Is that how you treat your guests? That isn't very polite."

"Are you the one who defeated these guards?"

"Oh! So you finally noticed! I might have had a hand in contributing to their current situation. I have to say though, they don't train city guards like they used to. They were honestly pretty weak..."

Shepherd let the man ramble for a bit before asking his question. "Where is my uncle?"

"Oh don't worry about him. He's safe, at least for now..."

Before the man could finish, Shepherd was triggered, thinking the man held his uncle hostage. He attempted to surprise the man with a quick swing of his staff but suddenly, the man disappeared from Shepherd's sight.

Anticipating his target would appear behind him, Shepherd turned around ready to attack but there was no one there.

"Ahem, to your right."

Shepherd turned to the right and saw that man standing nonchalantly. That enraged him further and he swung his staff again. Instead of just dodging, the man rolled under the attack and took out Shepherd's legs.

"Man, you might be weaker than the four soldiers."

That comment fueled his anger and he bounced back up and leapt for another strike. Feeling a bit less amused, the man elbowed Shepherd's stomach, forcing him to drop his staff. He then grabbed him by the collar and held him up against the wall.

"You want to see your uncle again, then you are going to do exactly as I say."

In the short exchange, Shepherd could feel the gap between their fighting levels. Even as he tried to break free, he couldn't. Seeing no other alternate option, he decided to stop fighting. The man let go of Shepherd and he slid down the wall, trying to catch his breath.

After he regained his normal breathing, Shepherd asked, "What do you want me to do?"

"Up on Mount Zion, there is a hidden tomb. There is an item there that I need you to retrieve."

"And what exactly am I looking for?"

He was about to walk away but he stopped for a moment to reply. "You'll know it when you see it."

As he stepped out of the room, Shepherd chased after him. He lost sight of him for a moment when he exited the door but when he stepped out, the man had completely vanished. There was no trace or trail left behind.

Shepherd was confused as to what was going on. Nothing made sense to him but he wouldn't have time to ponder as the unconscious soldiers were beginning to wake up. He made his way out and left before they were aware of his presence.

As he was leaving the farm, he took one last look back at the place where he had stayed for the majority of his life. He was going to leave behind the familiar and set foot on a new journey.

Chapter 5: False Champion

After all the commotion in the arena, Caleb found himself in a room filled with charts and diagrams showcasing the various fighters in the arena and also a schedule for future events. There were also low-quality trophies on the shelves along with many other vintage items, such as portraits that highlighted historical fights in the underground.

Sitting in a chair that was turned facing away from Caleb was the man who ran the entire operation. Hearing someone enter his door, he turned his chair around and put his arms on his desk.

"Ahhh the man and the legend himself of the underground arena, Caleb."

"You are too kind, Commissioner Haman!"

"Oh no, ever since you have arrived, profits have been on the rise. I can't thank you enough for your participation."

"Anything I can do to help and entertain the people."

"I heard there was a bit of an anomaly that occurred in your fight today."

"Yeah, some of the city soldiers showed up and my fight ended with a DNF."

"How unfortunate."

"No worries though, I'll get us back in the win column in no time!"

"Actually, there has been a change of plans. I would like you to concede your next match."

"Wait what? You just said profits have been on the rise because of me."

"Past tense. Your ratings with the audience are on the decline."

"That was just one fight. I promise after the next one I will..."

"Caleb, the people want a new champion and you are becoming old news. Now, do as I say, lose your next fight on purpose, understood?"

"Sorry Commish, I ain't going out like that. I'm going to keep fighting every battle until someone beats me when I give it my all."

His comment was met with a chuckle from Haman. "How rich."

"What's so funny?"

"You seem to be operating under a false assumption."

"And that is?"

"You think every fight that happens down here is a fair game."

Caleb was stunned in silence for a moment. "Wait, you mean my fights were..."

"Rigged, staged, scripted, yes. Call it whatever you like but that's the truth."

Suddenly, there was no reply from Caleb. He was trying to process everything Haman had just told him and wondering how much of it was true.

"Well, I never expected you to have nothing to say. Now, leave my office and be sure you remember what to do at your next fight. Oh, please do make it entertaining. The crowd always loves a good show."

"No." Caleb stood his ground and would not move.

"What did you say?"

"You heard me. I'm done with this. I'm no longer participating in anymore of your games."

"My my, you really are an amusing one. You think you have a choice in the matter." He pulls out a piece of paper and slams it on the desk in front of him.

"Umm, unless I'm a rock I don't see how that piece of paper is suppose to frighten me."

"I'll explain this so even a simple mind like you can understand. This signed document basically states that you are my slave and will do exactly as I tell you."

"I never signed such an agreement."

"No, but the one who left you here with me did."

"And who was that?"

"Tch, I don't have to tell you anything. Now, leave my office and follow orders."

"Fine, but can I just say something to you before I go."

Haman motioned with his hand to allow Caleb to speak his last words. However, Caleb wanted to make sure the commissioner heard him clearly. He leaned forward towards Caleb and when they stared each other eye to eye, Caleb spoke.

"Gotcha."

Caleb jabbed Haman in the windpipes and grabbed the paper that was on his desk. The commissioner needed a moment to recover and when he looked up, he saw Caleb had dashed out the door. He immediately called for his minions and commanded them to bring back Caleb alive with the document.

Hiding the paper in his pocket, Caleb ran as fast as he could through the underground area. He took a quick look behind to find a band of Hamans followers wearing brass knuckles trailing behind. He knew if they even caught up to him, it would spell impending doom. As he turned the corner in hopes of losing his pursuers, he collided with the woman who had her hood knocked off.

While Caleb was shaking off the collision, the woman quickly put back on her cowl before yelling at him.

"You really need to watch where you are going!"

"Sorry lady, I got no time to talk right now."

He immediately got up and continued running.

"Hey wait! I need to talk to you!" She followed after him.

Despite the delay, Caleb was plenty fast and still kept quite the distance away from his pursuers. He was approaching a large wooden door at the end of the path but there was someone there waiting, preventing him from passing.

"Let me through!"

"Sorry, no contestants are allowed to leave. Orders from the commissioner."

Caleb was extremely frustrated as he knew he didn't have much time. He needed a way out but he didn't want to harm the man in front of him to do it. But seeing as he had no choice, he was about to do the unthinkable, until the woman appeared.

"Oh, it's you again. Are you planning on leaving now?" Asked the doorman.

"Yes, thank you."

Caleb saw this as his chance to escape but the door guard would not allow him to pass. They could also hear the oncoming minions approaching to capture him.

"I'll just wait until they arrive." He said with a smirky smile.

"Why you..." Caleb was furious and wanted to clobber the man but the woman stepped in.

"He's with me."

"Sorry lady, but I can't let him out. Rules are rules."

She pulled out another bag of coins and gave it to the man. He opened it to check the contents. "Rules were meant to be broken!" He unlocked the door that had a complex opening sequence.

Caleb and the woman stepped out of the boundary and escaped into the city. The pursuers that were after Caleb stopped when they arrived at the door. They were unsuccessful in their mission and had to report back to Haman.

Chapter 6: Unlikely Allies

Entering the farmland was the woman dawning the dark cloth armour along with her mask. All the animals that were still there were feeling unease by her presence. They all gave a cry and then ran to distance themselves away from the stranger. The only animal that stood around was Ramsey.

She remained silent and gave off an aura that would cause most to cower away but the sheep slowly approached her. All the other animals that were witnessing from afar cried out for the sheep to run away but he continued to move forward. When Ramsey was within range, the woman quickly drew out her weapon and swung her katana at her target.

All the animals looked away, fearing the worst. However, when the animals opened their eyes, they saw that the woman's blade was pointing an inch away from the sheep's eyes. She was surprised by the creature's boldness and sheathed away her weapon.

She then turned away from the sheep and continued into the house, sparing Ramsey's life. Although Ramsey didn't flinch, all the other animals were all relieved.

Inside, the house was completely ransacked with no one left inside. It was clear her target was no longer here. Using her intuitive detection skills she examined the damage around the room.

In minutes, she figured out that there were four soldiers here that were trying to apprehend a man who lived in this house. However, someone intervened and defeated the four soldiers, rescuing the owner of the home. The owner then left, leaving the rescuer behind and shortly after, was when her target, Shepherd, entered the house.

Once she had his trace, she followed it out the house and saw footprints that lead into the forest. She followed Shepherd's footsteps and began tracking him down.

Lady Athaliah had just exited out of the lower floors of the castle where the dungeon was located. She was frustrated after her visit with a particular person but she was not allowing it to ruin her mood. She was hoping to have some time to gather her thoughts while she was in her room but to her dismay, there was a knock on the door. One of the commanders entered upon her permission.

"Lady Athaliah, I have news for you."

"This better be good."

"The runaway you sent for us to retrieve. Well, she got away..."

"Then why are you still here?"

"My apologies, my lady. We will continue our search."

"Good. Don't return until you have captured her."

Shortly after the first commander left, another soldier entered into Athaliah's presence with another report.

"Finally, I've been waiting for some good news. Where's the boy?"

"Uh... You see my lady, he somehow managed to get away..."

"WHAT?! You are telling me a measly shepherd boy defeated four armoured soldiers?"

"We believe he might have an acquaintance..."

"I thought the soldiers you have been sending have been well trained."

"They are."

"Then one extra fighter shouldn't make a difference should it?"

"No, my lady. I will be sure to send a higher quality batch of soldiers."

He then left the room and closed the door behind him. Athaliah's anger was slowly subsiding but her worries were now multiplied. She was stressing about all the events that were happening and how they could foil all the hard work she had put into her master scheme. She paced around until she felt an unsettling aura that made her heart sank. It was the ominous being that had his identity concealed by the shadows with a raven on his shoulder.

"Oh, it's just you..."

"My my, is that anyway to greet someone who has done so much for you."

"You left too many loose ends. The boy is still alive!"

"A minor inconvenience. Rest assured I already tasked someone to take care of this nuisance for you."

"What about the other one? Is he going to cause any problems?"

"I had him cast away as a slave. Even if he managed to become free somehow, he should be no threat to you."

She looks at herself in the mirror, checking for any wrinkles or blemishes on her face. "I guess I shouldn't worry too much."

"Exactly. Everything is going according to plan. You will have everything you desire soon enough." Those were his final words as he turned into a flock of ravens and disappeared.

After escaping from the undercity, Caleb was now staying at a room inside a local inn. There were two separate beds in this small room and Caleb was ready for a good night's rest but there was just one minor problem.

"Alright, you have done nothing but peek out that window constantly, while keeping yourself hidden. Don't worry about those scoundrels from the underground and get some rest."

"It's not them I'm worried about."

"Huh? Then why are you so paranoid?"

"It's... nevermind. You won't understand."

"Well duh, you haven't told me anything. Of course, I don't understand!"

"You are right."

"I am? Whoa, I didn't think you would admit defeat so easily." Caleb said in shock.

"I need your help."

"With what?"

She pulls out a scroll and places it in front of him. It was a map and she pointed to a place far out from the city. "This is Mount Zion. Think you can get me there?"

"Whoa lady, you do know that is not somewhere you just stroll into right?"

"I know it's going to be a difficult road. That's why I went into the underground arena. I needed to find a capable warrior who could help me reach that location. You are the reigning champion in the arena. Think you are up for the task?"

Caleb was hesitant as he was still mulling over what Haman said, about his fights being staged. "Hey listen, I'm not who you think I am. I..."

"No way, you are telling me that you are..." Caleb was thinking she would use the word fraud. "A COWARD!"

"What?! I'm no coward!"

"Then why are you hesitating?"

"It's... ugh, you won't understand."

"But that's because you haven't told me anything." Caleb gave her a death stare.

"Ugh, fine. I'll go with you on your stupid quest."

"Really?"

"Yes! Now go to bed!" He turned away as he got ready to sleep.

The woman was delighted to hear him accept her request. She finally left the window and lay on her bed about to fall asleep. As she was about to do so, Caleb had one last question.

"Hey, what's your name?"

"It's Alex."

"PFT! What?! That's a dude's name!" She chucks a pillow over and hits him in the head. "Oww."

After that exchange, they faced the opposite way, pretending to fall asleep. However, they both remained awake a while longer to do some thinking. Although it was going to be a difficult road ahead, they both had something to gain from this journey.

Chapter 7: Venom

It was getting dark in the forest but Shepherd wanted to make more ground before finding a spot to rest. The shadows combined with erie noises would cause many to be consumed with fear. Shepherd had some of the feelings but he refused to listen to them. He remained focused on moving ahead until he heard some rustling in the bushes.

He didn't think much of the noise at first until he heard it a second time, and then a third. Based on the time between each noise, he figured someone or something was following him. He walked forward again but this time, he remained vigilant to where the sound was coming from.

It would take a few more steps before the sound appeared for a fourth time. Shepherd immediately turned around and vaulted towards the bush where the sound appeared. He lunged through the bush ready to swing his staff but all he saw was a rabbit.

Thinking he was beginning to get paranoid, he decided it was now a good time to find a place to rest. As he turned around, he saw a human face that spooked him and caused him to fall on his back.

"No... It can't be... You are that guard... How are you alive?!"

There was no reply from the guard. His stare was blank and his skin was pale. All he did was slowly walk forward towards Shepherd.

Shepherd was overcome with fear that he couldn't get up and run. Instead, he tried to slide away using his legs to push off but it was no use. The man grabbed him by the neck and then held him.

Shepherd was gasping for air and he tried to get the man to let go. The man gave an insidious smile as he let go of his neck. Shepherd was relieved until he realized he was falling from a cliff. He could feel gravity pulling him down quickly as he fell into a dark oblivion.

It was right after the fall, that Shepherd snapped out of his slumber gasping for air. He looked around his whole body to find he had no injuries. He wiped some of the sweat away with his arm as he realized everything that happened was just a terrible nightmare.

Knowing he couldn't go back to sleep with his body drenched in sweat. He made his way to a lake in the forest to wash his face. As he was wiping his face, he looked down on the water and saw in the reflection, someone wearing a mask.

"Can I help you with something?"

She moved a little closer before suddenly drawing her sword for a pre-emptive strike. Despite how quick she was, Shepherd just managed to duck below the blade that sliced off a tiny bit of his hair. Then he reacted by splashing some of the water toward his opponent, hoping she would at least flinch. However, the enemy was not fazed, as she calmly sidestepped the water with little effort.

Seeing her reaction, Shepherd knew he was up against a highly skilled opponent as most fighters would overreact. He was studying his opponent and he noticed something off about her mask. He couldn't pinpoint what it was exactly, but he felt a disturbing energy emanating from it.

"You can help by staying still."

Judging by the sound of the woman's voice, he got the sense that she was older than him.

"Alright, you got me." He put his hands up as she slowly moved towards him.

Suddenly, Shepherd threw a few stones that he had picked up earlier when washing his face. Again, with a sense of calmness, the masked swordswoman deflected the stones aside with her blade. However, that was enough of a distraction that Shepherd was able to flee the lake and run towards the area surrounded by trees.

When the woman stepped into the area that Shepherd fled into, she kept quiet, listening for any footsteps or sounds. She knew he hadn't gotten far and that he was somewhere within this vicinity.

Meanwhile, Shepherd was hiding behind a bush, covering his mouth so his pursuer couldn't hear his breathing. He did his best to keep still while under immense stress but as he was monitoring his enemy, he began to hear a hissing noise. He looked on the ground to see that there was a snake near him.

To make matters worse, the assailant was approaching his way. He was caught in a dilemma, if he were to move now he would mean his end by the attacker's blade. However, if he were to keep still, he would be bitten by the snake, which was most likely venomous.

The footsteps were getting closer until they suddenly stopped. The silence and suspense were weighing on Shepherd, but suddenly, the blade appeared inside the bush. It had barely missed Shepherd in the hip. He reacted by rolling out of the bush and attempting to flee.

Unfortunately, the woman anticipated his movement and swept his feet the instant he got up. Shepherd fell back down and landed on his chest. He turned his body around and the instant he did, the woman stepped on his ribs and held out her sword near his face.

It was in this moment that Shepherd realized that this was possibly where it would all end for him. He quickly reminisced about what he did against the city guard. He was thinking this was retribution for his actions against another human being.

Shepherd had no will left to fight but he noticed something slithering towards him. It was the snake from back in the bush. It was making its way and about to strike the woman who swung her blade at it earlier. She was so focused on Shepherd that there was no way she could react.

"Look out!"

The blade wielder was caught off guard and she was frozen in place. Shepherd lunged towards her and pushed her to the side. The masked woman fell on her hip and she was furious at Shepherd until she saw what he had done. He took the fangs of the serpent on his right arm.

After the snake injected its venom, it was immediately sliced in half by the woman. With the slithering critter dealt with, she grabbed the tail before turning her attention back to Shepherd.

He was lying on the ground with his skin turning pale and his veins were popping out from his arms. It was a sign the poison was spreading through his body.

The woman now stood before Shepherd, looking down on him. Her objective was to take care of her target and she had a couple of choices. She could either finish him off with her weapon or let the poison slowly deteriorate his entire body.

On the contrary, she chose neither option. Instead, the masked woman put her sword away and tied up his wrist and legs with a rope.

"Hey! What are you doing?" She tightly secured the ropes and began pulling him along the ground.

"Owww, hey I can still walk you know."

"The poison will spread quicker the more you move."

"Oh... I guess that's a problem."

"It is. Now keep quiet and don't make me regret my decision."

After that reply, Shepherd no longer spoke another word and for a moment he noticed something different about his enemy. The dark energy he sensed around her mask had disappeared.

Chapter 8: The Deal

Back in the office hidden in the underground arena, the commissioner was receiving news about Caleb.

"You Imbeciles! You had him outnumbered and you still let him escape?!"

"He wasn't alone! There was this mysterious person hidden in a cowl and..."

"So you are telling me you and your six muscle heads couldn't capture two people?"

"Well yes, but..."

"OUT! LEAVE!"

His minion left the room with his head down. After he closed the door, Haman rubbed his head to get rid of an oncoming headache. Despite his hatred for Caleb, losing him in all the upcoming fights would be a detriment to his profits. He needed to find a competent mercenary to capture his slave back as he clearly couldn't rely on any of his minions.

He was about to go through a list until he heard a knock on the door. The sound caused him further frustration and he yelled for the person to go away. However, his words were ignored as a short man, about four feet tall, opened the door and entered his office.

"I told you to go... Oh, it's you, the one who hangs around the giant a lot. Sorry, what was your name? Lucas? Linus?"

"It's Liath actually."

"A strange name. Regardless, the fight schedule will be released soon. You can return tomorrow and..."

"That's not why I'm here commissioner."

"Hmm? Then what brings you to my office?"

"I can't help but overhear that you have a lost champion on the loose."

"Tch, so you know now? If you even think about telling anyone else..."

"I'm not here to blackmail you. I'm here to do business with you."

"Interesting. Speak."

"Golly wasn't satisfied with their battle and wanted to settle the score. We can track him down and deal with him. For a fair price of course."

Haman pulled out a blank piece of paper and using his feather pen, he wrote down a number and showed it to Liath. "How does that sound?"

"The commissioner is a very generous man. I will leave and tell Golly at once!"

"Wait." Liath stopped and turned to look at Haman again. "Bring him back alive."

"But sir, Golly doesn't know his strength, it would be very hard for him to control..."

"How about double the amount?"

"Oh, I'm sure I can get Golly to reconsider."

The commissioner smiled and the little man left his room.

Back in the castle, Lady Athaliah was about to visit someone. Along her way, she saw a soldier on the opposite side holding a basket containing some food. As they met at the giant wooden door that they were both about to enter, the guard bowed.

"Lady Athaliah, are you planning on speaking with the prisoner?"

"That is none of your business."

"My apologies."

"What do you have in your arms?"

"Oh, this? This is for the prisoner."

"May I have a look?"

Athaliah held out her hand expecting to receive the item. The soldier was fearing for what might happen if he refused. With his hands shaking, he handed over the basket to Athaliah. Inside was some rice with a small side dish of veggies. She immediately threw the basket on the ground, leaving the soldier stunned.

"My lady, that prisoner..."

"We are in the middle of a famine and you were giving away food to a low-life prisoner?"

The soldier became silent, not knowing what to say.

"Now, get out of my sight. I wish to speak with the prisoner alone." With his head down, he turned away from her.

Once Athaliah was alone, she opened the wooden door and descended down the stony stairs. The place was dimly lit by torches and filled with cobwebs on the corners of the walls. It was definitely the worst kept place in the entire castle.

She continued walking through the area, where she passed by many cells filled with different prisoners, all of whom she ignored. The one she wanted to visit was at the end of the path, isolated in a room away from the others. She had to open one final door and once she entered, she closed the door behind.

"Lady Athaliah visiting me again so soon? It must be my lucky day."

"Don't test my patience. You are lucky to still be alive. Now, tell me what I want to know."

"And what's that? You are going to have to be more specific."

"Tell me where she is going!"

"Who are you talking about?"

Athaliah slammed the metal bars as she lost her composure.

"Oh my, I didn't expect the great Athaliah to lose her temper so easily. That's not very ladylike of you."

"Enough!" She turned her back on the prisoner. "Let's see how that attitude of yours holds up after going a week without food." She left and slammed the door, which could be heard throughout the prison. She made her way through the halls and up the stairs where she saw the guard in charge of supervising the entrance, sitting around looking aloof.

When the guard saw Lady Athaliah, he immediately jumped and stood up for attention with sweat running down his forehead.

"You. Make sure that woman doesn't have any food for the rest of the week."

"But Lady Athaliah, that woman is one of the council members to the queen."

"Former council member. And don't question my authority again or you will join the prisoner and starve for a week."

"Understood Lady Athaliah."

She then walked away and returned to her room.

Chapter 9: The Slums

After resting the night, Caleb and Alex made their way towards the city gates. To avoid being spotted by the soldiers patrolling throughout the city, Caleb had to guide them through the alleys. Taking this route, they bypassed all the public traffic and soldiers but Alex wasn't prepared for what she was about to witness in this area.

Hidden in the alleys away from the eyes of the city were the less fortunate who had nowhere to go. Many of these people were dressed in rags with less-than-ideal hygiene. Some were low on money, some were sick, and the famine only exacerbated their problems.

"Don't make eye contact and keep walking." Caleb quietly told her.

However, Alex's eyes caught the sight of a little girl with pale skin, who was coughing profusely. All she had witnessed was too much for her to bear, so she immediately went to the child who was near her mother.

"Hey stop! What are you...?"

When Alex was next to the child and her mother, she kneeled to their level. "Your child is sick, you need to take her to a doctor and get her some food!"

"I would love to, but I don't exactly have the luxury to do so..."

Alex reached for a pouch and pulled out some coins. "Here, take these and get some food for the both of you and some medicine for your daughter."

"Oh bless you child!"

As the woman received the money, Caleb rushed in and grabbed Alex.

"Hey, what's your deal?"

"Just what do you think you are doing?"

"I'm trying to help people who are in need."

"You can't just give money to someone you don't know! Especially not in a place like this."

"Unlike you, I have a heart."

"That's not what I meant. Argh! Why is it so hard to talk to you!"

Their argument would have continued but someone shouted at them in the alley. "Hey, that's the woman with money!"

"Maybe she will give us some money too if we ask."

All of a sudden, the mob of commoners began to swarm towards Alex. She was confused about what to do and her legs would not move. Thankfully, Caleb grabbed her by the arm. "This way!"

Caleb led the way and Alex followed behind with the crowd chasing after them. As the chase continued, it was clear Caleb could easily outpace their pursuers but Alex was falling behind. Not only was Caleb moving further ahead, but the people were closing in.

Noticing that Alex's endurance would not hold up, Caleb took a turn at the next corner. Alex did the same but right after she turned around, Caleb grabbed her by the shoulder and pulled her back. Alex was confused but Caleb signalled for her to stay quiet as they hit behind the giant trash bin.

As the crowd turned the corner, they continued running forward, thinking that's where Alex and Caleb had gone. Instead, the two waited patiently for the stampede of people to subside. When the sound of footsteps had disappeared, Caleb carefully surveyed the area.

"Alright, I think we lost them. Let's get going before they figure out we gave them the slip."

Caleb began walking but as he took a few steps, he couldn't hear any footsteps following him. He turned around and saw Alex standing still with her head down.

"Hey, what's wrong? Was it something I said?"

"I'm sorry for what I said to you earlier. About you having no heart."

"Oh, that? Yeah, don't worry about it. I've been called far worse things."

"It's not only that. I didn't know what would happen when I gave the family the money. Sorry for making your job more difficult."

"Well, if you are really sorry, then you will quit apologizing and start walking."

"Oh, I can do that!"

She snapped out of her melancholic state and began to follow Caleb. The two of them continued through the alley, and this time, Alex made sure to listen to Caleb.

Pulling up to a small town just outside the forest, Shepherd was getting dragged to a small medicine shop by the masked woman. Before entering the shop, she placed Shepherd in the side alley.

"Stay here, don't move or..."

"Or the poison will spread fast, yeah yeah you mentioned that many times on the way here."

"Well if you would listen, I wouldn't have to repeat myself."

"You try staying still while getting dragged around everywhere!"

Interrupting them was a homeless man who couldn't ignore their bickering. "My my. I've never heard a louder brother and sister argue so loudly in all my life."

"What?! This big bully is not my sister!"

"Ugh, no way. I wouldn't be caught dead being related to this immature brat."

"What did you call me?!"

The old man rolled his eyes and attempted to go back to sleep. The woman gave Shepherd a light kick in the ribs.

"Oww, what was that for?"

"No reason. But if you move from this spot when I return, I'll make sure that kick will be twice as painful."

Shepherd was furious but there was little he could do. He was stuck with a homeless man, who was trying to sleep. Shepherd thought this would be the longest wait of his life until he heard some footsteps approaching his way.

When the store owner heard someone entering his shop, he fixed his posture to greet his customer.

"Well, good afternoon today. How can I be of service?"

"I need an antidote for a snake bite."

"You are going to have to be more specific than that young lady. There are many types of snakes and each one has..."

She pulled out the tail and threw it on the counter. "Is that specific enough?"

"Oh my... Give me a moment, I will see what I have in the back."

When the man returned, he put some herbs into the mortar. Once all the ingredients were inside, he used the pestle to mash all the ingredients together. As he continued with the process, the woman had a question for him.

"Judging from your reaction to the snake tail I showed you earlier, that creature must be venomous."

"Well, I'm not certain as there are two kinds of snakes that share that same colour scheme. One is non-venomous, but the other could potentially be life-threatening if not treated in time."

He finished mixing the compound and was now putting the mixture into a bottle.

"So how long before the venom spreads and becomes incurable?"

"One day."

He handed the bottle over to the woman and she paid him by leaving the proper amount of coins on the counter. She then immediately left the shop without saying another word.

Once outside, she immediately walked to the alley where she left Shepherd. "You are quite lucky, it seems there is plenty of time before the poison..." She paused as Shepherd had disappeared.

She looked around the area but found no one except for the sleeping homeless person from earlier. With haste, she forced the man to wake up from his sleep.

"Oh, it's you again. Why can't you leave a poor homeless man alone?"

"Where is he?"

"Huh?"

"The boy who I left lying here."

"Oh, a few men in armour took him."

"Men in armour?"

She was momentarily confused, but after some thought, she realized they were most likely soldiers sent from the city. Thinking they couldn't have gone far, she was going to chase after them blindly, until she looked down on the ground where she placed Shepherd.

She lowered herself and picked up what appeared to be a piece of sheep's wool. It most definitely belonged to Shepherd, and as she looked a bit further down, she saw another piece lying there. So she followed the trace, sensing it would lead her straight to Shepherd and the soldiers who abducted him.

Chapter 10: Manure

After being captured by a group of four soldiers, Shepherd was now forced to walk with his wrist restrained. To compound his problems, the poison had not been cured from his body and was only going to get progressively worse. In combination with fatigue, he was starting to feel the effects of the poison. He grew lightheaded and fell on his side.

"Hey, get up and keep walking!"

Shepherd attempted to get up on his own but he would stumble back on the ground. The group leader rolled his eyes and got two of his subordinates to assist him. The two guards each grabbed one of his arms and pulled him up. He got back on his feet but his balance was still shaky.

"Alright, that's enough standing still. Let's get a move on."

He pushed Shepherd and got him to move along. They all continued walking along the plain towards the city. However, unbeknownst to the guards, Shepherd falling to the ground was part of his plan. While they were so focused on helping Shepherd get back up, they didn't notice that he dropped behind his left sandal.

Caleb and Alex had made their way and were now within viewing distance of the city's border entrance. They could see people lining up, waiting for their turn to be screened by the soldiers to determine whether they were allowed into the city.

"It seems like many people are being turned away. Is this normal?" Alex commented.

"No, it's most likely the famine that's making it so difficult. Lucky for us, we are leaving this place so we should have no problem just walking through!"

"Umm, we can't do that."

"Huh? Why not?"

"Look at how many soldiers there are! I'll definitely get caught if we try to walk through."

"Seriously, what kind of crime did you commit?"

"It's... complicated. Sorry."

"Sigh, yeah yeah. But we still need to figure out a way to go through that gate."

They seemed to be at an impasse but as they were still pondering, Caleb heard a noise coming from a building nearby. He went to see what it was and he found a person rolling a bunch of manure on a wagon out into the back alley to discard it.

"Ewww, that smell is gross! What is that?"

"Our ticket out of here!"

One by one, people at the gate were being turned away from the city. Even families with little children were refused entry as the soldiers stuck to their strict protocols. As they continued to deny entry, Caleb, was rushing out with a wagon towards the soldiers.

He was wearing a hood over his head and covering the content of his wagon was a giant cloth. It looked as if he was going to barge through the gate but one of the soldiers signalled for him to stop.

"What is your reason for leaving the city?" asked the inspecting soldier.

"I'm a merchant and I'm looking to sell my goods elsewhere for more profit."

"You aren't smuggling any food beyond the city walls are you?"

"No sir."

"You better not be lying. You would not be the first to think of such a strategy to get rich as we have caught many and thrown them in prison."

"I assure you, that you will find no food inside this cart."

One of the soldiers went up to the wagon and lifted the cloth. The instant he did so, a horrendous stench rushed into his nose. The scent was so strong, the other soldiers and even some of the people in line could smell the stench.

"By the heavens, what is that smell? And what kind of merchant are you?!"

"Oh sorry, I forgot to say I sell fertilizer for a living."

"He sells feces for a living!" One of the soldiers yelled.

"Yes, thank you for clarifying. Send the man through!"

The soldiers were stepping aside and allowing Caleb to wheel his wagon out of the city. He was so close to leaving without any trouble or interruption when suddenly, he heard someone yelling his name.

"CALEB!"

"Oh shoot..." It was the muscle heads who worked for Haman. They were angry at Caleb for making a fool out of them and they were out to seek revenge.

After hearing his name, one of the guards paid closer attention to his face. "Caleb? Wait, it can't be! You are Caleb from..."

"Nope! You are definitely mistaking me for someone else!" Caleb was now urgently trying to escape but the other soldiers were now blocking his way. "Hey, I thought you gave me the okay to leave!"

"That was before we found out that you are associated with those buffoons. Men, lock him up!"

Caleb was in a dilemma and he could see no possible way out. He raised his hands to surrender to the guards but suddenly, the cloth on the wagon popped off. Alex appeared and began throwing manure at the soldiers. It spattered right in their face, hindering their vision momentarily.

"We are really sorry about this." Alex told the soldiers as Caleb knocked them aside with the wagon.

"She is, I'm not!"

Caleb continued pushing the wagon with Alex on it, covered in the stench of manure. They got past the soldiers but they were not out of trouble yet. There were still Haman's lackeys chasing after them.

"They are gaining on us!" Alex yelled as she saw the enemies drawing closer.

"Well this wagon is kind of heavy."

"Are you calling me fat!?"

"No, the manure all over the cart is though."

"Oh."

She then grabbed more of the repulsive dirt and threw it at their pursuers. It was much more difficult to throw on a moving wagon, so Alex's aim was not as accurate as before. However, the weight on the wagon was decreasing, meaning Caleb could pull them quicker. He did not stop and once he ran past a wooden sign, all the lackeys suddenly stopped and didn't chase them any more.

"Why did you stop? Aren't we going to capture them?" One of them asked but the other pointed to the sign. After they all read what it said, they grew silent.

"They won't survive the night. No point in risking our lives."

So they all turned back into the city.

Chapter 11: Split

Within the royal palace, Athaliah was going through a plethora of dresses. There were three female servants handing her the different outfits. She was trying them on and looking at herself in the mirror to see which one would be best.

"Hmmm, how does this one look?"

The three looked at each other, afraid of saying the wrong thing. However, one mustered up the courage to speak. "It looks wonderful on you Lady Athaliah." She said in a nervous tone.

"Excuse me? What did you just say?"

"Ummm, I was just saying your dress looks very nice on you and..."

"No not that. What did you call me?"

"Lady Athaliah?"

"Exactly. One of these dresses is going to be for my future coronation. I will no longer be addressed as 'Lady,' but rather as Queen Athaliah!"

"But isn't the queen returning to..." She didn't finish her sentence because the other two servants were signalling for her to be quiet.

Athaliah was now seething with anger and she was about to give the servant lady the scolding of her life. However, she was saved when a soldier entered the room.

"Lady Athaliah, I have urgent news to report. Some good and some bad."

"Let's start with the good."

"The good news is that we located the runaway woman near the border of the city."

"And let me guess, the bad news is you let her escape?"

"Yes... I'm terribly sorry my lady."

"How incompetent can you and your men be?"

"We ran into some complications. The runaway appears to have an accomplice."

"Tch, one extra person is causing you all this much trouble? How worthless." She now had her back turned to the soldier and was about to go back to looking at the dresses.

"One of the guards got his name. I believe it was Caleb."

Suddenly, Athaliah stopped and her eyes were wide open. "What did you say his name was?"

"Caleb."

After hearing his name, she felt a pit in her stomach. She had to take a deep breath to calm her nerves before replying to the guard. "You are lucky you caught me in a good mood. I'm giving you and your men one last chance. Send your best soldiers and bring them both back to me."

"Both?"

"Yes, the runaway and that Caleb character."

"As you command."

The soldier left the room, leaving Athaliah with her servants. However, after the news she received, she was no longer in the mood to try out the various dresses. She commanded her servants to leave her alone and they did as they were told.

When she was the only one left in the room, she went to her closet and looked for an outfit that would not draw much attention. She needed to travel outside the palace and speak with someone about their current problem.

After eluding both the soldiers and Haman's lackys, Alex and Caleb were alone in the marshlands. Needing to get rid of the foul stench,

Alex went to wash off in the lake while Caleb sat around the vicinity and looked away.

"You know we would get there to your destination a lot faster if you were quicker."

"Excuse me?! Whose idea was it to cover me in manure?!"

"Hey, I wasn't hearing any other ideas coming out of your mouth!"

"Oh you always have something to say don't you? I'd bet that's how you get yourself into trouble all the time."

"You got a lot of nerve saying that after getting a whole mob to swarm after you in the alley. How could you be so clueless and naive? You've probably been pampered and spoiled your entire life."

"Me? Pampered?! Spoiled?! Well at least I'm not some brainless muscle-head who hasn't been taught any manners by his mother!"

After hearing the last comment, Caleb had enough. "You know what? I'm out of here. I don't need to deal with your disrespect. Go up that mountain yourself." He got up and began walking away.

"Fine! I will!"

After Caleb had stomped off, she continued to stay in the water until most of the stench vanished. When she was finished, she got out of the lake and put on a new set of clothes. Then, she got a campfire going and sat near it to keep warm.

She tried to think about anything other than the argument she just had with Caleb but it would not leave her mind. The more she tried to forget, the more the thought grew and kept replaying in her head. She was in a tough conversation with herself.

"Argh, he's so inconsiderate!"

"But he did save me from the mob."

"He came up with that stupid plan on purpose so I would be covered in that foul smell!"

"But it was honestly a pretty smart idea..."

"How am I going to get to Mount Zion, I don't even know where I'm going."

"Maybe he will come back. But what if he doesn't?"

"Sigh, maybe I should go look for him and apologize."

She continued to contemplate at the campfire, battling with her thoughts.

Meanwhile, Caleb was walking through the marshlands by himself with similar thoughts. He too couldn't erase the argument he just had with Alex.

"Argh, she's so critical about my ideas."

"But, she does have a good heart."

"Maybe she does need my help to get to that mountain..."

"Nope, she can figure it out herself!"

"But she's all alone out here."

He was still contemplating on his next course of action, until he heard footsteps in the distance. Caleb used his surroundings as cover and slowly approached the scene where the noise came from.

Where he was hiding, he counted three soldiers and a teenage boy who was under arrest. He kept hidden and monitored the situation to gather more information.

"Hey?" One of the guards spoke to his comrade.

"What is it?"

"It's the prisoner. Is he supposed to look that pale or sweaty?"

Together the two soldiers stood up and moved towards Shepherd. One of them squatted down and got a closer look at him.

"Hey kid, something wrong?"

"Poison..." His voice was very faint and the soldier barely heard the word.

"Poison?"

"Maybe he got bit by something?"

"Perhaps, or he could just be acting and trying to pull a fast one on us."

"What should we do?"

"Let's wait until the commander comes back. I'm not taking any chances. If we mess things up, Lady Athaliah will have our heads."

As Caleb heard that name, a strange feeling seized his body. "Athaliah? Why does that name sound so famili.." However, Caleb became distracted by his thoughts and he didn't notice someone sneaking up behind him and knocking him behind the head. He fell to the ground unconscious and got dragged out of bushes.

The soldiers were waiting around until they heard footsteps approaching near them. They stood for attention as they saw their commander had returned.

"Commander! We have urgent news to discuss. Wait what do you have over there?"

He throws Caleb on the ground in front of them. "Another prisoner to add to our collection."

Chapter 12: Shepherd and Slave

Alex was now wandering through the marshlands by herself in search for Caleb. She followed the direction she thought he went but despite how long she had been walking, she saw no sign of him. She regretted her decision to argue against him until she heard something rustling nearby.

She immediately turned around but there was nothing there. She exhaled thinking she could calm down but when she turned back to her original direction, she saw a masked person right in front of her. The sudden sight spooked her to fall on her bottom.

Alex was in a bit of pain but that was secondary to what was before her. A masked woman with a blade on her back was walking towards her. She wasn't sure of her intent but the woman gave off a malevolent aura.

"I'm looking for some city soldiers. Have you seen them?"

"I have not." Alex was nervous but she did her best to conceal it.

"How unfortunate." She was about to walk away but Alex had more questions.

"Wait, what do you plan to do once you find them?"

"They took something that doesn't belong to them. I will see that they get their punishment." She said that with her hand on the handle of her blade.

"If that's the case, then I can't let you do that."

"Oh, and why not?"

"Because they are good people who have families and friends to take care of."

"Interesting. And what are you going to do to stop me?" By now, she had her blade pulled out and was walking closer to Alex.

"I believe I can help you get back what they took from you."

"Ha! Those are bold words." She laughed initially but then she saw the look of determination on Alex's eyes. "I see you are serious. Tell me then, how will you get back what they have stolen from me?"

"Let's work together and find them first. After that, I promise they will return what is yours without any need for senseless bloodshed."

"You are an interesting one. Alright, I'll play your game for now."

So for the time being, Alex followed the woman as she tracked down the soldiers who were holding Shepherd captive.

Meanwhile, Caleb was just waking up after being hit in the back of the head.

"Ugh... What in the world hit me? And why am I all tied up?"

"Isn't it obvious?" Caleb looked over and he saw a teenage boy tied up not too far from him.

"Okay wise guy, care to tell me why we are tied up?"

Before Shepherd could speak, he was interrupted as the soldiers along with the commander appeared.

"Well well, so glad you are both conscious now."

"You... you were the one who hit me in the back of the head!" Caleb shouted.

"Very perceptive. The rumours they say about you are true, Caleb."

"How do you know my name?"

"It literally says your name on one of your tattoos on your arm."

"Oh right... Wait, what do people say about me?"

"Nothing much. Just that you are a warrior fighting in the scum of society. Which is like nothing more than a slave."

Caleb was about to jump at the commander but two of his soldiers restrained him. One held him down his lower body while the other one pressed his chest to the ground. However, the commander still wanted to speak with him so the guard lifted Caleb's head to see the commander's face.

"You can't keep me tied up forever. Just you wait, when either you or one of your guards slip, I'll..."

"Yes yes, I know all about how crafty you can be. Lucky for me, I don't plan to keep you around much longer."

Caleb was confused but Shepherd interrupted their conversation. "What do you plan to do with the two of us?" He said weakly as the poison was still coursing through his body.

The commander looked at Shepherd. "Well first, we are going to deliver this slave back where he belongs. I can't believe someone would be willing to pay such a hefty amount to claim this low life."

"Haman..." Caleb said quietly to himself.

"What about me?" Shepherd asked.

"I fear for you my boy. You will be handed to one of the most terrifying people known to human existence. Lady Athaliah."

"Lady Athaliah? That name..." Shepherd had a thought but suddenly he began coughing uncontrollably.

"Hey are you okay?" Shepherd couldn't reply with words as his cough continued. "He's not looking so good. You got to help him!"

"Tch, what a lousy attempt. You can't fool me with such a simple trick." The commander turned away but his two soldiers attempted to reach out to him.

"Uh commander, we think they might be telling the truth. His skin is looking extremely pale and..."

"Don't be a fool! It's clearly one of their tricks so they can catch us off guard and give us the slip but I refuse to fall for it. Go grab them, we are moving out!"

Chapter 13: Name

The two women continued walking through the marshlands together. There was a huge contrast in their demeanor as Alex was vigilantly alert for danger. While, the other woman walked calmly with confidence.

"You don't get out much, do you?"

"How did you know?"

"Your movement and body language says it all. You are constantly paranoid and think anything in this place can harm you."

"But anything can! This place is full of stuff that can hurt me! Wait, how are you so calm?"

She stopped walking for a moment so she could explain to Alex. "It's all about selective attention."

"Selective what?"

"Basically you learn to pay attention to only what's important and forget about everything else. Let me demonstrate." She began walking over to Alex. "Just breathe."

Alex closed her eyes and inhaled a deep breath in before exhaling it all out. She did it a few more times as the woman continued her explanation.

"Right now you can focus on all the aspects of your breathing and ignore everything else. By cutting off your sense of sight, you enhance other senses in your body. Now open your eyes."

Alex opened her eyes and she realized her focus was no longer on her breath but on everything else she was looking at.

"Now you aren't so aware of your breathing because your sight is focused on something else." She was continuing her speech but she was walking closer to Alex with her hand on her blade. "With enough training, you can control your senses to ignore what's irrelevant." She now drew out her sword and held it near Alex, who was nervous. "And what can possibly end your life." As she said those words, she drove her blade towards Alex's face. Alex closed her eyes fearing the worst but when she felt nothing for a few seconds, she slowly opened her eyes.

Alex saw the woman holding the blade near her shoulder and then pulling it away from her. Slowly, she sheathed her weapon back and began walking away. Alex was confused until she looked on the ground and saw a spider that was the size of a human hand, lying on the ground. She pieced it together, that it was the woman who had saved her from the eight-legged creature.

"Hey wait up!" The woman continued walking slowly so Alex easily caught up. "Thank you for saving me from that arachnid."

"You should learn to pay attention to your surroundings better. You might not be so lucky next time."

"Could you tell me your name?"

"I...uhhh...I don't exactly have one."

"What? That's not possible, everyone has a name! What do your friends or family call you?"

"I don't have any."

"Oh, well we can be friends then!"

"You would do that for me?"

"Yeah of course, but we really need to give you a name."

"You have any idea what my name should be?"

"Hmm, well there is a 'W' on your mask, and you move really quick like the wind. How about Windsor?"

"Windsor?"

"You don't like it? We can change it to something else."

"No, it's a good name. I'll keep it. Thank you."

"You are welcome Windsor!"

All of a sudden, Alex felt the change in Windsor's energy. No longer could she sense darkness around her but rather a spirit that was much brighter. Similarly, Windsor also felt a transformation, feeling as she could trust Alex. They were beginning to enjoy each other's company but their moment would be short-lived as they heard a noise further ahead. Not certain what it could be, they moved together to identify what made the sound.

In a hidden dark alley within the city, Lady Athaliah snuck her way into the area without anyone noticing. She was waiting alone until someone appeared.

"Well well, if it isn't Lady Athaliah. I didn't think I would see you again so soon."

"Cut the pleasantries. Tell me Commissioner Haman, is Caleb still under your possession?"

"There's been a minor issue but I'm working on a solution..."

"So you somehow managed to lose him! The incompetence!"

"You are the one to talk, you let the queen slip right through your hands."

"Silence! That is not how you speak to a woman of royalty!"

"Ha, you ain't the queen yet. And with the way you act, you will never be queen."

Those words triggered something within Athaliah and she was about to lose her tantrum but a dark shadowy being began to form near them. Its face could not be seen but its overwhelming presence could be felt. When it spoke, it was in a low tone and would cause normal humans to shiver in fear.

Immediately, both Athaliah and Hammon stopped arguing and paid attention.

"Quit your bickering. Our master would not be pleased."

"Tell that to the witch."

"Me?! You sleezy..."

"Enough! Despite both of your folly, everything is still going according to plan. There is little chance of them stopping what's about to transpire."

"The master has nothing to fear. I have sent a good mercenary to take care of that Caleb." Haman assured the shadowy figure.

"Excellent. Even if that fails, I have a trump card that will assure our victory. Now, return to your assignments and make sure you don't squander anything else."

The shadows disappeared leaving only Athaliah and Hammon in the alley. They looked at each other with disdain, before going their separate ways. Hammon returned to the underground, while Athaliah went back to the castle.

Chapter 14: The Queen

With chains around their wrist, Caleb and Shepherd continued walking through the marshlands, followed closely by the soldiers. They had been on the move for quite some time, until Shepherd suddenly collapsed on the ground. Caleb stopped and checked on him.

"Hey are you alright?"

Shepherd was in so much discomfort that he was unable to reply. His body was sweating despite the temperature not being warm. Caleb called for the soldiers to help him. One of the guards moved towards Shepherd who was lying on the ground. He kicked Shepherd in the ribs.

"What are you doing?! Can't you see he's in no condition to walk!" Caleb shouted.

The soldier reacted by kicking Caleb in the chest. "Silence knave, know your place."

Caleb was furious after getting hit and was ready to retaliate. He charged towards the soldier despite being restrained and having no weapon. The commander and the other two soldiers stood back and watched the show as their lone comrade was about to pull out his sword. He wanted to discipline Caleb and show him no mercy.

However, before the man could even draw out his weapon, the fight was over. Caleb stopped in his tracks and watched as his opponent had fallen to the ground. The commander and his two lackeys were speechless as they slowly looked at the person who took out their ally. It was the woman with the mask, Windsor.

"Hey! Who do you think you are?" One of the soldiers yelled but she never replied. Feeling insulted by her silence, he drew his sword out and ran towards her.

As Windsor was about to strike, Alex ran into the battlefield to get her attention. "Please don't hurt them! They are good people, but they are just misguided."

"No promises." In an instant, Windsor dashed away and engaged in battle.

While everyone's focus was diverted away from Caleb, Alex appeared near him.

"Long time no see. How have you been?" Caleb jest.

"You are in no position to be making jokes. Now stay still and keep quiet so I can find a solution to these chains."

"Uhh these things are made of metal. You are going to need the key."

"I knew that..."

"Sigh... This is a failed attempt at a rescue."

Their comedic situation would have continued until something was thrown before Alex. She picked up the item and saw that it was a set of keys. They both looked to see that it was Windsor who had thrown them after dealing with the two soldiers with ease.

"Whoa, she's good." Caleb commented.

"Yeah, I'm glad she's on our side."

Alex found the right key and unlocked the chains on Caleb. He moved his wrist and arm around, after having his movement restricted for so long. He was ready to find the commander and get his revenge but he wasn't in sight.

However, after seeing how the situation was unfolding, the commander held Shepherd close to him with his sword near his neck.

"Drop your weapons." He demanded.

Windsor held her blade out, ready to strike. Caleb was assessing the situation to see if there was an opportunity to save Shepherd. However, neither of them made the first move.

"Enough!" Alex spoke up and walked towards the commander. "No more fighting. Let him go and you can take me as your prisoner instead."

"You are the runaway that Lady Athaliah wants arrested."

"Yes. Present me to her and leave everyone else here alone."

"A one for one trade? That hardly seems fair. Especially if you are in no position to be making trade demands."

Windsor and Caleb were both growing impatient as they could see Shepherd's condition getting worse. Alex could sense that they both wanted to attack the commander but she held them both back.

"Both of you, please drop your weapons."

"Are you crazy?! He's going to take both you and him away!"

"Trust me, just this once."

Caleb wasn't happy with the situation but despite his emotions, he decided to listen to Alex. He told Windsor to drop her blade and although she struggled, she obeyed.

"As you can see commander, I've asked my friends to drop their weapons. Take me as your prisoner and leave that young man behind."

The commander struggled to make the decision so Alex pulled out her last card.

"I know this must be tough for you commander. So I'll make this easier for the both of us." She took down her hood and revealed her face to the commander.

"You... You're..." Caleb and Windsor were confused as the commander dropped to one knee. "Queen Alexandra."

"Queen?" Both Caleb and Windsor stared at each other in confusion.

Alex walked towards the commander and asked him to stand up. He slowly got to his feet as Alex had much to ask him.

"Tell me, how are things back in the castle?"

"Ever since your mysterious departure, it has been nothing but turmoil. Not only is the food ration being depleted because of the famine, but Lady Athaliah has made everyone's life a living nightmare. She is never satisfied with any of our efforts and no one is willing to stand up to her. To make matters worse, she's going to be crown queen, if you don't return soon!"

"I see. I'm sorry you and everyone had to endure through all that. I thought leaving the castle would help the situation but I can see it only made things worse."

"What are we to do now?" Asked the commander.

Alex looked at everyone and took a deep breath to gather her thoughts. "Ready your men commander. I will be returning to the city with you."

The commander was shocked by her response, but he never questioned her as he saw the determination in her eyes. He bowed to the queen and attended to his soldiers who were injured by Windsor.

Alex then turned to face Caleb and Windsor who were left wanting answers.

"Say what?! You were the queen this whole time?!" Caleb exclaimed.

"Yeah... Sorry for keeping that from you."

"And you are leaving halfway through your quest? The fun was just getting started."

"Sorry, I have to cut our journey short. I know this is asking a lot, but could you head to Mount Zion for me?"

"Uhhh, I don't even know what to do once I'm there..."

"I'm not asking as the queen but rather, as a friend."

"You sure? It really sounds like you are pulling that queen card right now."

"So you aren't going to do it?"

"Well I can't exactly go back to the city so I guess I'll go."

Alex was very appreciative of Caleb's response as she turned to face Windsor. "I have a favour to ask of you."

"You want me to accompany you to face Lady Athaliah?"

"No, she is someone I have to face on my own."

"She sounds far too dangerous, I should..."

"I have a more urgent request. Please."

"What is it you ask?"

"Go with Caleb to Mount Zion."

Windsor was speechless when she heard the request. She had no idea how to respond. "I.. He... How..."

"I know we have just met and I'm asking a lot, but I feel you are someone I can trust."

There was much going on in Windsor's mind. She never came to a clear conclusion but Alex had no time to wait for her. The commander and the soldiers were waiting, so she hugged Windsor.

She then gave one last thank you to both Caleb and Windsor. She wished them the best and hoped they could save the boy who had been poisoned. With their final exchange of words, she followed the commander and his soldiers back towards the city where she would face her adversary, Lady Athaliah.

Chapter 15: New Trio

For the moment, Caleb was sitting alone at the campfire with his thoughts. He was trying to process everything that had happened and how he ended up in his current situation. He kept thinking until Windsor sat down beside him.

"How is he?"

"I gave him the antidote and his temperature is slowly getting back to normal. He should be fine, but he won't have his full strength for a while."

"So what are we going to do with him? We can't just leave him here all by himself."

"I was dragging him around before with a rope."

"You what?! That could have given him burns and more injuries!" Caleb yelled.

"He wasn't complaining. Not that I would stop if he did."

"Dragging him along the ground is no longer an option."

"What do you suggest we do? Carry him?"

"Actually yeah, I could carry him on my back no problem."

Windsor shook her head. "You would have to carry him up the mountain. With the air pressure combined with the extra weight, it will be far too difficult."

"Well I'm going to do it, just watch me!"

As Windsor rolled her eyes, Caleb turned around hoping to find Shepherd but he had disappeared. They both were in a panic thinking someone else might have kidnapped him while they weren't paying attention. With haste, they were about to search for tracks to follow until they heard someone clearing their throat.

"Ahem." It was Shepherd who was standing but holding onto a walking stick.

"Kid! You are alive!" Caleb shouted and punched him in the shoulder.

"Please don't call me that."

Windsor walked up to him and surprised him with a punch to the gut.

"Owww, what was that for..."

"For making us worry. Don't do that again."

"I was trying to rest, but someone was being loud and kept talking." Shepherd directed his comment at Windsor.

"That wasn't me!" Windsor yelled back and they looked ready to scrap.

"Sheesh, if I didn't know any better I would have thought you two were siblings."

"WE ARE NOT RELATED!" They yelled simultaneously.

"Okay you two calm down, I was only joking."

After that comment, Caleb was preparing to leave.

"So what's everyone's plan?" Caleb asked the two of them.

Shepherd took the initiative. "I have to head up Mount Zion."

"Wait, what? You are in no condition to hike up that mountain!" Caleb exclaimed.

"Why is this a problem? You said earlier you would carry me up the mountain."

"That is true, you did say that." Windsor confirmed.

"Argh, I like it better when you two fought against each other. So what about you?" Caleb's question was directed at Windsor.

With her arms crossed, she replied, "Well, someone has to keep an eye on the two of you."

"HEY! I'M A GROWN MAN!"

Both Caleb and Shepherd yelled to defend themselves. They then stared at each other for a moment but while they were distracted, Windsor had already started walking.

"Are the two of you just going to have a staring contest or are we going to move?"

"Race you there!" With haste, Caleb left Shepherd in his dust.

"Hey not fair, I'm still healing!"

And together, this unlikely trio began their journey towards the ascent of Mount Zion. However, little did they know, they were being monitored and followed.

Chapter 16: Mount Zion

Up on Mount Zion, a heavy snowfall had occurred, blanketing the entire terrain with sheets of snow. Scattered through the area were Musk Oxen traversing through the cold land. Other than that, there wasn't much of a view thanks in large part to the terrible winter conditions.

As the oxen were minding their own business, a little man sat on the shoulder of a giant, thinking about their next move.

"Hey Liath, why are we here? Shouldn't we attack and smash our target?"

"Patience Golly. It's going to be difficult right now as he has recently acquired some allies."

"The puny teenagers? Does Liath think Golly is weak?!"

"By gosh no! I just want to eliminate all external variables before you fight your most hated opponent."

"Oh, what does that mean?"

"I want to make sure it's a fair one on one fight with no interference."

"Oh! Liath smart. Good plan! I like! But what do we do?"

"Sigh, just keep watching. I'll tell you what you need to do." Golly listened to his friend and walked in the direction of the oxen.

As the giant and the little man were up to their schemes, Caleb, Windsor, and Shepherd continued venturing through the mountain. The snow was hindering their mobility but they were determined to find their target before nightfall.

Shepherd still hadn't made a full recovery and continued to hold onto his walking stick. Despite that, he was able to keep pace with Caleb and Windsor.

Caleb kept looking back to check on Shepherd in case his strength gave out. However, while he was looking back at the young man, he noticed Windsor had stopped. He found her standing at the edge and walked up to her.

After asking her why she suddenly stopped walking, Windsor pointed down below to where Caleb should direct his attention. What he saw was the entrance to the tomb that Alex was talking about.

"That must be the tomb that Alex was talking about!" Caleb announced.

"Seems like it. We should keep moving. If we make it down quickly, we won't need to find a cavern to camp in."

As Windsor was about to head off, Shepherd stumbled. "Sorry. I don't think my body will be able to keep up. Would it be okay to rest for a bit?"

"We have been traveling without a break for quite some time. How are you feeling Windsor?" Caleb asked.

"I'm fine." She said with a stern voice.

Caleb looked back at Shepherd and then came to a decision. He spotted a cave nearby for everyone to rest. Shepherd was very thankful while Windsor seemed more irritated but followed anyway.

After they got inside the cave, Caleb got a fire started. He was about to ask Windsor for help but when he turned to her, he found her fast asleep and didn't want to wake her. He was about to get up himself until Shepherd appeared with some extra sticks he found inside the cave. He handed them over to Caleb and then joined him.

"That was pretty clever."

"What are you talking about?"

"You can drop the act now. You knew how tired she was didn't you? But you knew she was too stubborn to admit it, so you pretended to complain so she could rest."

"I may or may not have done that."

"Got a high EQ there."

"Thanks, I have my uncle to thank for that."

"Sounds like a great guy. Where is he now?"

"He is being held hostage by someone."

"What?!"

"Yeah, the man who took him told me that if I wanted to see my uncle again, I needed to head towards the tomb in Mount Zion."

"That explains why you wanted to follow Windsor and me towards the mountain."

"I just hope after all this he actually gives me my uncle back."

"Hey, I don't know who this guy is, but if he dares show his face around me, we'll beat him up together."

"Are you serious?"

"Yeah of course. Between the two of us, there's no way we could lose!"

Shepherd was baffled because he never told Caleb how deceptively quick the man was. However, whether they would beat the man in a fight was irrelevant. Shepherd was more moved that there was someone who was willing to help him who wasn't his uncle.

"Uh hello? Anyone there?"

"Oh sorry, I was lost in thought. Thank you."

"Alright, looks like you need some rest too. Go sleep, I'll take watch first."

As Caleb was about to stand up, Shepherd took notice of his tattoos. "Hey what are those?"

"Oh these? They are tattoos I got a while back."

"What's that one?" He pointed to one that had clouds with some lines on it and near it was some fire.

"They are actually two separate tattoos but they go well together. This one is the wind which represents freedom, and the one next to it is fire, which symbolizes passion."

"Oh, so they represent who you are as a person."

"Yeah..."

"Huh? You sound uncertain."

"Well I know what they represent, but I can't remember the exact reason I got these."

"Oh, I'm sure you'll remember one day."

"Thanks, I hope so too. It's been bugging me."

"Hey, what's that one right there?"

"Haha, funny you saw this one. This one is a shepherd standing beside his sheep. The shepherd is a symbol of a person who protects those he cares about."

After explaining his tattoos to Shepherd, Caleb went to stand guard near the entrance of the cave. Shepherd slowly rested his body on the ground but before closing his eyes, memories of what happened to his uncle replayed in his mind.

"Protector huh? Well, that ain't me."

He then rolled to his side and closed his eyes.

As Caleb stood inside the cave entrance monitoring the surroundings, he wasn't aware that he was being watched from afar. Golly and Liath had tracked Caleb and the giant was eager for revenge.

"Now we go?" asked the giant.

"No. Give it until morning. That will be our opportunity to strike."

Chapter 17: Golly Liath

Waking up alone in the cave was Windsor. She looked around hoping to find Caleb and Shepherd but neither of them were around. She figured they were standing guard at the entrance together so she was about to move there until she heard an ominous voice further into the cave.

Unable to ignore it, she travelled further down the cave alone where the atmosphere got darker and more eerie. Windsor was not terrified as she was confident in her fighting abilities but she felt a weird feeling on her face. She had never been able to take off her mask before but something caused her to give it an attempt.

She put her hand over the mask and slowly it came off without much resistance. Something about her face felt off so she looked around to find a small pond. When she got there, she slowly put her face over the water. She was expecting to see her reflection, but the water turned black and red and she saw an unsettling human with long hair.

"No... That can't be me..."

She tried to escape but vines from the ground emerged and wrapped around her arms and legs. She fought with all her might but it was no use as she was dragged into the pool of darkness.

Windsor suddenly woke up from her nightmare. Caleb was near her as he was checking to see if she was okay from all the screaming. However, instead of responding verbally, Windsor attacked Caleb and tossed him away.

Shepherd had just woken up from his sleep and the first thing he saw was Caleb flying past him. He ran out to check on Caleb immediately after his impact against the snow.

"Hey, are you alright?"

"Yeah, I'll be fine. The snow lightened my fall."

"What even hit you that hard?"

Caleb pointed and when Shepherd looked inside the cave, he saw Windsor standing. However, this was not the same Windsor as the one he had gotten to know. Instead, he could sense a dark aura from the mask, similar to when he first encountered her.

"Oh no."

"Has this happened before?" Caleb asked.

"Yeah, when we first met, she actually wanted to strike me down."

"What?! How did you get her to change her mind?"

"I don't know! There was a snake that was about to bite her but it didn't because it bit me instead and..."

Before he could finish his sentence, Windsor reappeared with her blade in her hand. With haste, she was about to swing her weapon at both of them, but Caleb reacted by kicking Shepherd out of the way and then jumping away himself. Caleb was lying on his back and as he opened his eyes, he saw Windsor slashing down the blade towards him. Thanks to his reflexes, he drew out his sword and parried her weapon.

"Windsor snap out of it. I don't want to hurt you."

He was restraining his strength and because of it, Caleb was getting pushed back. His own sword plus Windsor's blade was closing in on his face. The edge was an inch away from his nose when suddenly, Shepherd jumped on Windsor's back and held onto her. That forced Windsor to move away from Caleb as she was struggling to get Shepherd off her back.

Caleb was slow to get up, but once he gathered himself, he was ready to help Shepherd. However, as he was about to take the first step, he felt the area rumbling. He scanned the area and his eyes led him to the hills where he could see a herd of musk oxen stomping down. He then looked to where Windsor and Shepherd currently were.

"Oh no..." Immediately he dashed towards them.

Windsor threw herself on the snow and knocked Shepherd off. Shepherd was attempting to pick himself up but he was kicked in the ribs. When he opened his eyes again, Windsor was standing over him with her blade held in front of his neck. He closed his eyes as Windsor was about to drive her blade at him, but she stopped when they felt a rumbling in the area.

Stampeding towards them was a small herd of musk oxen. They both stared at the charging animals as they were paralyzed by their confusion.

The approaching herd was appearing fast but rocks were pelted at their head causing them to run more wildly. Caleb had further angered the herd but as they were moving in random directions, all of them ran around or away from Windsor and Shepherd. The two had avoided disaster but a few of the oxen that Caleb provoked charged towards him.

"No! Get out of the way!" Shepherd yelled.

However, Caleb was too exhausted from the lack of sleep and the amount of energy he had exerted. The oxen collided against him.

Seeing the impact, the dark aura shrouding Windsor's mask dissipated and she snapped back to her senses.

"Caleb!" She turned to Shepherd. "We have to go after him!"

Shepherd wasn't sure what happened but he was relieved to see Windsor return. They were about to search for Caleb but impeding their way was the giant and the tiny man on his shoulder.

"Finally, Golly can get his revenge on little man and..." The giant took a closer look by hunching down. "Hey! Where is little man?!"

"It looks like my plan worked too well. The stampede must have gotten him."

"What!" The giant began stomping the ground in frustration.

"No worries Golly, I'm sure the herd couldn't have taken him too far. Let's search the area."

Golly was about to turn around begrudgingly but as he did, he was met with Windsor who stood with her weapon in hand. She overheard everything they said and was now furious about what they had done to Caleb.

Sensing her ill intent, the giant reacted by trying to grab her but he wasn't expecting her to be so quick. She avoided his hand and swung her blade against his arm. When the metal made contact against his skin, she felt some resistance. Looking at his arm, she saw that he only suffered minor cuts. She was going to need an alternate form of attack as this opponent's skin was far tougher than any she had tried to cut.

However, before she could formulate a new strategy, Golly slammed his arms at Windsor, which she avoided. He followed up with another arm swing and this time she barely dodged getting hit.

Shepherd was watching the battle unfold before his eyes. He knew Windsor was at a huge disadvantage not because of her size, but because her speed was severely restricted. The snow and cold weather was hindering her movement far more than the giant. He needed to find a way to help Windsor that wouldn't interfere or make the situation worse.

The fight continued with Windsor trying to find a weakness but unable to do so. Golly threw a punch in her direction and although she was ready for it, her foot got caught in the snow. Seeing this, the giant thought he had the battle in the bag but Shepherd jumped in and pushed her out of the way.

They had both avoided the giant's fist but with Shepherd lying down, Golly switched his attention to his new target. He clasped both his hands together and slammed them where the boy was. A flurry of snow flew into the air upon impact, and when Windsor saw what transpired, she retaliated against the giant.

Somehow, her speed had increased and Golly was on the defensive. She swung her blade with great precision and agility, which caused the giant problems but Liath was not fazed.

"Ha, this won't last, she will get tired and then she's ..."

He was cut off as Shepherd snuck up onto Golly's shoulder and grabbed Liath from behind.

"Hey what?! You're that annoying pest from a second ago! How are you still alive?"

"Ha, your brute friend never touched me. All he did was smack a bunch of snow, which provided the perfect cover for me to sneak on."

"Pretty clever, but you aren't winning! Golly, on your shoulder!"

The giant reacted by dusting off his shoulder. His finger had enough strength to flick both Shepherd and Liath off him and they both landed on the snow. As that was happening, Windsor located a part of the giant's anatomy that she could strike, his knee. She slashed the right knee area and the giant roared in pain.

With Windsor being so close, she was caught in the giant's roar and had to cover her ears from the sound. Because of this, she wasn't focused on Golly, who began swinging his arm wildly, knocking Windsor aside.

Shepherd managed to pull himself out of the snow and was hoping to get back to help Windsor. To his dismay, he saw Windsor struggling to get up. In addition, he witnessed Golly picking up Liath, who was injured. Once his little friend was safe on his shoulder, he approached Windsor.

"Windsor get up!" He yelled, but she could barely move after the last impact.

Golly towered over the helpless woman and he was ready to deliver the finishing blow. He had his arms lifted but as they were raised, Liath heard the sound of galloping approaching towards them. He attempted to tell the giant to check his surroundings but before they knew it, Golly was rammed into by a musk ox with a rider on it, Caleb.

"Argh, thought I got rid of you already." Said the disgruntled little man.

"Sorry, I'm not that easy to get rid of."

"We'll see about that. Golly push back!"

The giant attempted to plan his feet on the ground as he grabbed the horns of the ox to slow it down. Caleb looked behind Golly and saw a cliff behind the giant. He encouraged the ox to continue pushing, hoping to push them off.

With Liath's encourage, Golly's endurance increased and the ox couldn't push him further. Caleb looked around for options and noticed the giant's knee was still bleeding. The wound struck by Windsor earlier was his new target. He pulled his sword and threw it towards the afflicted knee. When Caleb's weapon struck the giant's knee, the giant lost focus as he yelled in pain.

The ox gave one final push and successfully got Golly over the cliff with Liath on his shoulder. However, he wasn't going to fall alone. The giant attempted to take Caleb down with him by grabbing the ox's horn.

Caleb attempted to grab onto the edge but it was out of reach. He could feel his body falling and was trying to figure out how he would survive this fall but someone grabbed his right arm. Shepherd had lunged forward and was holding onto Caleb's arm.

"Hold on! I'll pull you up!"

Shepherd was lying in an awkward spot and couldn't get much power to lift Caleb back onto the cliff. Caleb could see Shepherd's strength starting to give out and if he didn't let go, there was a chance both of them could fall.

"Shepherd let go. If you hang on any longer we will both fall."

"No, I can do it!"

Seeing Shepherd's determination, Caleb reached with his left arm holding to grab on but instead, Shepherd lost his grip and Caleb's right arm slipped out. Shepherd had a sinking feeling in his gut when he saw what happened. He watched as his friend's hand slipped out of his grasp but out of nowhere, someone grabbed Caleb's left arm.

"Windsor!"

"A little help please." She said in distress.

Shepherd grabbed Caleb's right arm and together with Windsor, they pulled Caleb back onto solid ground. All three lay on the ground exhausted but after a moment of rest, they sat up and looked at each other. They couldn't help but laugh after everything that had just happened. They each helped each other up and continued on their way towards the tomb.

Chapter 18: Royal Reunion

Athaliah was trying on another dress with her servants in the room. She kept looking at her outfit in the mirror and changing her angle, making sure it was perfect from every view. While she was focused on critiquing her dress, a soldier entered and asked to speak to her.

"This better be good."

"Lady Athaliah you have a guest who wishes to see you..."

"Ahem, that's Queen Athaliah."

"My lady, the coronation hasn't happened yet and..."

"How dare you! I'll have you thrown to the wolves for your insolence! GUARDS!"

Four guards appeared before her and she recognized them from before. "Oh it's you four. I thought I sent you to go after the runaway. Have you returned empty-handed?"

"Actually Lady Athaliah, we found her."

"ITS QUEEN! Why does nobody get it?!"

"Maybe because you aren't the queen." Walking in was Alex and upon her entrance, all the servants reacted simultaneously.

"Queen Alexandra!"

Shortly after, soldiers throughout the palace marched into the room and stood to the side while the two women continued their confrontation.

"Well well, look who finally decided to grace us with her presence."

"This ends here Athaliah. I will not allow you to continue to oppress everyone in this city."

"Oh tough words. You and what army?"

"This army. Guards arrest her!"

At her command, the four soldiers who brought Alex in were advancing towards Athaliah. However, after taking a couple of steps forward, over half of the soldiers that arrived into the room all simultaneously drew their spears and stomped one step forward. They forced the soldiers that were with Alex to back away.

Meanwhile, Alex was puzzled by how the other soldiers reacted.

"You seemed confused. Almost like you expected all your pawns to listen to your every word."

Alex tried to hide her face, but she was worried and couldn't understand why they would still listen to Athaliah. "What did you do to them?"

"Me? Hahahahaha, how naive. Have you forgotten how you abandoned everyone during their time of greatest need? With the famine spreading throughout, you suddenly left without any explanation."

"I..." She tried to defend herself but Athaliah would not allow it.

"The famine only got worse after you neglected your responsibilities and guess who had to clean up after your mess?" She walked closer until she was near Alex. "Yes, it was me. I made sure everyone here would not starve. That is why they are no longer loyal to you."

Alex took a deep breath before responding. "I know what I did was wrong, but that is why I am here. Your torment among my people can no longer be tolerated."

"Oh, is that a challenge?"

"The one who falls will be banished and never be allowed to return."

"An intriguing offer, but unfortunately I will have to decline. My coronation is happening in the next few days and there is nothing you can do to stop it. Guards arrest her."

The majority of the soldiers were on Athaliah's side while the small minority stood in between to protect their queen. Assessing the situation, Alex saw no way out and she didn't want to sacrifice the lives of the soldiers who were defending her.

"Wait." She held out her hand and Athaliah allowed her to speak. "If I surrender myself, will you spare these soldier's lives?"

"Ha, how noble of you. Fine, I don't want needless bloodshed to sully this room."

Alex allowed herself to be taken as the soldiers placed shackles on her wrists and legs. They were about to escort her towards the dungeon but Athaliah had one thing to say to her. She whispered in her ear and suddenly, Alex was filled with rage. She headbutted Athaliah to the ground and was about to attack her but she was restrained by the soldiers.

"What did you do to her!? Tell me where she is!"

Everyone was appalled as the queen's composure had suddenly changed. Everything was going according to Athaliah's plan.

"The queen has lost her mind, she just tried to attack me! Take her to the dungeon at once before she hurts someone else."

Alex would not calm down but the soldiers had restrained. They pulled her away but Alex continued to be fixed on Athaliah. The deceptive woman pretended to be hurt but when she saw Alex's angry glare, she snuck a malicious smile that only the queen could see.

When the queen was no longer in sight, Athaliah stood up and wiped her bruises feeling no pain. There were the servants and some of the soldiers still standing and staring, not knowing what to do.

"What are you all just standing there for? Back to work! There is much preparation that needs to be done for my big day!"

As the servant quickly ran back to their responsibilities, one of her soldiers spoke to her. "What do we do about the traitors?" He was referring to the guards who were on Alex's side.

"Put them in the prison and make sure they get no food for the week. See if that changes their manners." Her soldiers did as they were told.

During the night, on the boundaries of the city gates, an outsider dressed in dark cloth armour snuck into the city through the underground sewers. Normally, there would be guards patrolling the perimeter of the city but years of this monotonous work caused some soldiers to be less attentive.

Once the man entered into the sewers, he made his way through until he came into a fork in the path. He looked in both directions and had a flashback of what happened before.

Uncle Joash was inside his home preparing food when someone made an unexpected arrival into his home. Joash was on his guard until he saw the face of the hooded man.

"Well well look who finally decided to visit. It's been a long time, which I can only assume means we don't have much time."

"Unfortunately you are correct. We can't wait any longer. We have to make a move."

"But Shepherd, he's still so young..."

"He will be fine. You have kept him safe all these years and he will be more than capable."

"I sure hope you are right. What do you need me to do?"

The hooded man threw a scroll at Joash, who caught it with his right hand. He then unravelled it and wasn't sure what it was. "What is the meaning of this?"

"It's a map of the sewer system. You can use this to navigate through the city undetected."

Joash was in shock. "How did you get your hands on this?!"

"Don't worry about that detail. Now, go save her. She has waited long enough."

"Thank you." Joash left the farm.

Shortly after was when the soldiers attempted to ambush Joash within his home but were instead met with the mysterious hooded man who made quick work of them.

Joash took a moment to pull out the map and after carefully surveying the area, he held his light source forward and continued moving on.

Chapter 19: Trials

After traversing through the mountain, Caleb, Windsor and Shepherd made it to the entrance of the tomb. The area looked ancient, filled with giant statues of people and creatures they did not recognize. What was more impressive, was how the longevity of the structures as they were still standing despite the extreme weather conditions on the mountain.

At the entrance, there was a mysterious man waiting for them.

"Welcome, I've been expecting the three of you."

Caleb and Windsor were confused by the man's comment and didn't know how to respond. However, when Shepherd heard the voice, he could recognize it instantly. His eyes widened and he pointed emphatically at the man.

"You! Give me back my uncle!"

"This guy took your uncle?" Caleb looked at Shepherd who confirmed his question.

Windsor was ready to draw out her sword but the man held out his hands with open palms. "I'm not here for hostility. You are here to seek the treasure that is within this tomb, correct?" Caleb nodded. "Then I suggest you save your energy. The trial that awaits will require your full attention."

Shepherd was still enraged and not listening but Caleb held him back and Windsor spoke up. "What about his uncle?"

"As promised, after you complete the trial and obtain what lies at the end of the tomb, he will see his uncle again."

They all considered their options. Having no idea what lurked inside the tomb was risky enough, but there was also no telling if the man would be true to his word. However, since they gave their word to the queen that they would enter the tomb, they made their choice.

"We'll play along with your game for now. But when we return with the treasure, you better free his uncle, or else I will show you no mercy." Windsor threatened.

The man chuckled. "Then it is settled. I bid you good luck on your adventure." He then disappeared from their sights, allowing the three to enter into the tomb.

Once the three moved inside, a stone door appeared and closed upon their entry. Caleb went to try and open it but upon slamming into the door without any effect, he came to the conclusion that there was only one way to go, forward.

Knowing they couldn't exit the same way they entered, they focused on the current room they were in. It was in the shape of a rectangle without much to look at other than the stone walls and a few skeletons lying throughout. There was a circle made out of stones and near it was some writing on a stone tablet. Shepherd began reading it out loud.

You begin with three,
But only two are free.
Sacrifice is key, a soul must remain,
To guard this room, their loss is your gain.
For two to pass, one must stay,
Only then will the path give way.
Follow the rules, and two will leave this room,
Cheat, and the one will surely meet their doom.

"So what does it say? I don't speak riddles." Caleb called out.

"One of us needs to stay behind or the door won't open." Windsor answered.

Caleb walked over to the circle of stone and made some observations. "I'm guessing this is where one of us will stand once we make our choice."

"Wait, you aren't seriously thinking about splitting up are you?" Shepherd was shocked.

"Relax, I'm just checking it out. Separating would be ill-advised if we can avoid it. We would be playing right into that guy's hand."

Windsor took a look at the distance between where the door to the next room was to the circle of stones. Then she examined some of the skeletons on the ground. "I'm guessing this is the remains of those who tried to break the rule."

"Grrr, there has to be a way..." Shepherd was growing frustrated but suddenly Caleb interrupted.

"Alright, I think I have an idea."

Windsor and Shepherd were surprised but before they could ask for details, Caleb told them to stand by the stone door. The two waited and when Caleb saw that they were ready, he stepped into the circle. After a short moment, the stone door began to slide down, opening a way through.

Windsor stepped over to the other side first, followed by Shepherd. They then turned around having no idea what Caleb had up his sleeve. Before leaving, Caleb dropped his sword onto the circle and then dashed towards the exit.

"What is he doing?! He's breaking the rule which means he will..." Shepherd was thinking about the threat of the riddle and fearing the worst for Caleb.

"He's pretty clever." Windsor said.

"What?" Shepherd was confused.

"He left his sword behind as weight to keep this door open. He's betting on the fact that this room won't know the difference between him and the sword."

Both Shepherd and Windsor were impressed but more importantly, it looked as if Caleb was going to outsmart the trial and make it through the door with them. However, a trapdoor appeared beneath him as he was about to take his next step. Unable to stop his momentum, he dropped down unable to be seen.

The two were appalled by what happened as the stone door was beginning to close. Windsor reacted by attempting to jump back into the room hoping to go after Caleb. She would have made it through but Shepherd held her back.

"What are you doing? Let me go!"

"The room is going to close! If you go back you'll end up like those skeletons there!"

"We can't just leave him!"

"I know... but..." The two were in turmoil until they heard Caleb's voice.

"It's okay." They were glad to hear his voice, as he was barely holding onto the ledge. "Go on without me, I'll find a way back to you guys. I promise."

"Come on Windsor, we have to move on."

With much reluctance, she gave in. "Fine. You better keep your promise!"

So Windsor and Shepherd continued on as the door closed, sealing Caleb by himself. After being left alone in the room, his strength gave out and he let go of the ledge and fell into the dark abyss.

When Caleb woke up, he saw two children appear in his mind. He could hear their voices but he could only see their backs. He called out to them and when they didn't hear him he walked towards them. As he got closer, the two humans suddenly disappeared and in their place was a sheep being blown away by the wind.

Caleb was confused but as he saw the sheep getting further away from him, he shouted, "Wait!" Then suddenly, everything went dark. He couldn't see anything as he wandered aimlessly and fell. In his confusion, he grew frustrated and slammed the ground with his fist.

Even though his hand was beginning to hurt, he continued what he was doing as he didn't have any alternative ideas. It was in his darkest moment, that some of the tattoos on his arm began to glow. Two in particular, the sheep and the wind. It created a light which showed a path. Despite not knowing where the path led, he stepped forward and suddenly found him awake in the tomb.

Caleb had finally returned to reality but he had no recollection of how long he had been unconscious for. All he knew was that he had to find Windsor and Shepherd urgently. He saw a glimpse of the two's dilemma in the next room. He had to intervene before they made an irreversible mistake.

Shepherd and Windsor had been walking through the corridor of the tomb until they stumbled upon a room which had another riddle. Beyond it was a large stone door that seemed impossible to be moved by sheer force. Windsor went to survey the room to see if there was another way while Shepherd read the riddle.

"The treasure you seek is not of gold,
But of memories of old.
To unlock the past and know its tale,
One must give, and another must fail.
Who will surrender, who will fall,
For only through death are memories recalled?"

When Windsor returned from exploring the room, Shepherd told her about the riddle.

"All this work for some memories? What a letdown."

"Windsor!"

"Relax, I'm only joking."

"So what are we going to do?"

"I don't think we are going to outsmart the system, based on our prior experience. So I guess one of us has to be the scapegoat."

Shepherd hesitated for a moment before replying. "I'll do it."

"Okay." Windsor responded without a second thought.

"Wait, you are completely okay with that?"

"Yeah, you just volunteered for it. What's wrong?"

"I thought you would at least try and argue against it!"

"No way, I'm not going to be the sacrifice, you can do it."

Shepherd couldn't believe Windsor's response. He thought Windsor would be more empathetic but he was mistaken. Not wanting to go back on his word, he went through with his decision. Windsor directed him to where he should stand. He begrudgingly listened and when he was standing where he was told, he braced himself for the worse.

He closed his eyes as a glowing light formed around him. It grew brighter, before surrounding his body but suddenly disappeared. Shepherd opened his eyes and looked at his hands. He was still able to move and he felt very alive. He was confused as to what happened until he saw a glowing light radiating from a different part of the room. He looked around and when he realized Windsor had disappeared, he dashed towards the light.

"WINDSOR!" As he yelled he turned the corner and saw Windsor standing in the circle with mysterious markings. He jumped towards her, hoping to stop the ritual but a magical barrier repelled him against the ground. Despite failing, he was going to try again but Windsor held out her hand to stop him.

"No, it only needs one of us."

"You didn't fight me about this a few minutes ago. Why the sudden, wait... You knew about this circle didn't you?" She nodded to his question.

"When I explored this room while you were reading the riddle, I figured out this was the spot you needed to stand on."

"So you let me think I was going to be the sacrifice knowing I would stand in the wrong spot..."

"I'm sorry for lying to you, but I knew you would be against my decision."

"But why?"

"I have done some horrible things throughout my life. But you Shepherd, you are a good person. The world needs more people like you."

When she said those words, he was reminded about what he did to the guard in Mahlon. "No, I'm not letting it take you!"

Shepherd was ready to jump at Windsor again but suddenly, a chain wrapped around his entire body. Shepherd was pulled down and lying on his back, unable to stand.

"Shepherd!" Windsor cried out.

Appearing in the room was the little man who always hung on Golly's shoulder, Liath. Although he had bruises and scratches all over his body, he had a nasty grin on his face as he held the chain tightly, making sure Shepherd couldn't move.

"You... survived?" Shepherd was weak but his voice could still be heard.

"That's right. And just like how you forced me to watch Golly fall to his demise, I will make you watch your friend suffer until her final moments. Then after, I will claim the treasure within this tomb!"

Liath continued to laugh as he watched Shepherd struggle. His attention was so fully absorbed, that he was upended from his blind side. Shepherd was still tied up but as he looked up, he saw who had saved him, "Caleb!"

His body was still aching from the fall. "I'll keep him distracted, go get Windsor."

Shepherd got out of his entanglement with haste and ran to where Windsor was. Then, Caleb turned around and faced his nemesis who harboured a deep hatred for him.

"Heh, so you survived. No matter, I was hoping for a rematch. Don't underestimate me. Just because I don't have Golly around doesn't mean I can't beat you."

"I'm very aware of that."

"Oh? How so?"

"Golly might be big and strong, but you are the mastermind behind everything. Plus, Golly is pretty much blind. Without you, he would walk aimlessly and trip over his own feet."

"Hoho, you are smarter than you seem. But enough chatter, I can't stand the sight of you so let's end this now!" Both fighters ran towards each other and clashed in the middle of the room.

Shepherd slowly approached the magical barrier and attempted to pass through it. However, he was met with much resistance as he was struck with magical shocks.

"What are you doing? You have to stop now!"

"No, we are not leaving you!"

"Caleb is losing his fight, you have to go help him!"

"He'll be fine. He gave me this chance to save you and that's what I'm going to do!" Shepherd continued to push against the barrier despite the amount of pain he was in. Windsor could only watch as there was nothing she could do.

Caleb was now on one knee and breathing heavily. His energy was nearly depleted and his enemy was walking towards him, holding a dagger in his hand. He tried to get back up on his feet but his entire body felt heavy. Liath ran up and tackled him against the ground.

Caleb was now lying near where the riddle was written. Liath held out his dagger and pointed at his nemesis' face.

"Psh, look at you. Champion of the underground fighting arena? Hardly. You had everything given to you with those staged fights. I had to struggle since the day I was young. Being the smallest, I had to fight for everything. A fraud like you could never beat me."

Caleb continued to struggle as he looked at Shepherd and Windsor. He saw that they were both in the ritual circle, potentially being offered as sacrifices. As Liath was about to stab Caleb with the dagger, Caleb grabbed Liath's wrist.

"What? What's going on?"

"You are right. I'm a fraud and you totally could have beaten me. But you made one fatal mistake."

"And what might that be?"

"You messed with my family."

Suddenly, Caleb picked up Liath and threw him against the stone pillar. Liath was hit hard but he was far from finished. In contrast, Caleb's burst of energy was depleted and he was now defenseless. Liath was not going to make another mistake but before he could move, a glowing circle suddenly appeared beneath his feet.

The little man was clueless for a moment but then he remembered the familiar glow. He realized he was about to be the sacrifice.

"What? No! This can't be happening! Please, help me!"

Even after all he had done, Caleb couldn't stand to see his enemy being sacrificed. He reached out his hand but it was too late. Liath's body was being taken away by the ritual circle and in mere seconds, his whole body vanished as did the mysterious glow. With his nemesis defeated, the adrenaline left Caleb's body and he was falling due to exhaustion.

He would've landed hard on his head but he could feel someone had caught him. Despite how weak he was, he had enough strength to open his eyes.

"Shepherd is that you?"

"Yeah, it's me. Don't worry, I think we finished all the trials. The tomb isn't trying to kill us anymore."

"Where is your sister?"

"Windsor is okay, she's right over... Wait, what did you say?!"

"Windsor, she is your sister."

"How? But... Wait. Did you know this all along?"

"No. After I fell in the other room I somehow had some of my memories returned to me."

"This doesn't make any sense. What is this place? We got to get out of here and..."

"Hey Shepherd, I'm exhausted so I'm going to take a short nap. Stay out of trouble alright son?"

"Wait what? Stop, don't go to sleep yet! Caleb!"

He was left with so many questions but Caleb was now fast asleep. Shepherd was a bit relieved knowing it wasn't anything serious but his mind was racing with so many thoughts. Not wanting to disturb Caleb's recovery, he ran over to Windsor.

"How is he?"

"Don't worry he's just resting."

"Thank goodness."

"Windsor, Caleb said something really weird just now. I think he might have hit his head too hard from the fall. He said you are my sister. Crazy right?"

"Shepherd... I think Caleb is telling the truth."

"What?! Alright, you must be going crazy after being in the ritual circle thing. Let's..."

He was interrupted by the sound of someone clapping. Shepherd grew angry as he saw that it was the man from the entrance of the tomb.

"Well done. You have survived and completed the trials. You have claimed the treasure that has been locked away in this tomb where many failed. It's great to see your family reunited. Well almost, just a couple of people are missing."

"Where is Uncle Joash?" Shepherd asked angrily and was about to attack the man but Windsor stepped in.

"I apologize for my brother's actions, he still doesn't have his memories restored yet."

"Brother? Stop playing around Windsor!"

The man calmly pointed to the circle where Windsor was earlier. "Step into the circle and all will be made clear."

Shepherd was skeptical but when he looked to Windsor, she let him know that it was safe. When she had her assurance, he slowly made his way towards the circle. Once his whole body was inside the boundary, a magical light began to glow and memories began rushing to his mind.

Chapter 20: Rescue

Deep in the dungeon of the castle, Alex was locked away alone in her cell. She was isolated from all the other prisoners and hadn't had any visitors. It was difficult for her to tell how much time had passed as she had not seen any sunlight. She thought today would be like any of her days in prison until the door began to open.

"Well well, look how the mighty have fallen. Once known as the Great Queen Alexandra and now reduced to this."

Alex was feeling weak as she wasn't given much sustenance during her time here. Lady Athaliah ordered the guards to give her only a small ration of food and water to keep her alive. However, despite her lack of nutrients, she still found the strength to speak.

"What did you do to me?"

"Oh? You wouldn't believe me even if I told you."

"You erased parts of my memories. There are things I can't remember."

"Well if you really wish to know, I made a dark pact."

"You what?! Please tell me you didn't!"

"See, I knew you wouldn't believe me."

"No Athaliah it's not that. You have to stop what you are doing, your life is in grave danger..."

Athaliah slapped her in the face. "Silence! I've spent too long under your shadow but all that is finally about to change. Tomorrow is the long-awaited day, my coronation." She paused, imagining how she would feel at that moment. "Oh don't worry, you will have the best seat for such an event. Right after my coronation, I will hold a special event in your honour!"

She never told Alex what it was as she was going to keep it a surprise until tomorrow. Athaliah was now about to walk away but Alex was not finished.

"Wait! Tell me what you did with my family."

"Don't worry, I haven't done anything to them, yet."

"You monster, don't you dare..."

"As long as my coronation goes smoothly and you listen to everything I say, then no harm will befall them. However, make any attempt to stop me, and you will never see them again." The door slammed shut, leaving Alex alone to grieve.

On the other side of the prison from Queen Alexandra's cell, security had been lowered as many guards had been relocated through the castle to prepare for the coronation. It was here that one of Queen Alexandra's most trusted council members was kept.

She continued sitting and waiting in her cell like any other day, until she heard a noise below her. She looked on the ground and noticed a metal cover inside her prison cell. The cover was removed and someone appeared to rescue her.

"Joash!"

"Shhhh, keep it down! Are you trying to get us caught on purpose, Kels?"

"Oh right, sorry!" She drastically decreased the volume of her voice.

"Alright follow me, we are getting you out of here!"

He reached out his hand and she gladly accepted it as they escaped through the sewers together. As they were walking through the foul stench, Council Member Kelsey spoke up.

"Hey Joash."

"Yeah?"

"Thanks."

"There is no need to thank me. You had to endure for such a long time..."

"All good. I knew you would come get me."

"What made you so sure of that?"

"I would haunt your soul for all eternity if you didn't."

"Fair point. On a more serious note, did you get any information on where that witch is keeping the child?"

"Yup, I got her to cough it up!"

"Alright, let's go get her."

While sneaking through the sewer system, they were able to move through undetected by any of the castle's security. In addition, Kelsey knew the layout of the castle having been here for so long. Together, they reached an isolated room that very few people would ever consider venturing into. There were no guards around the area, which made it less suspicious to the human eye.

Joash and Kelsey entered the room, where they were met with no resistance. The place looked like a guest room within the castle except it had compiled some extra dust and cobwebs as the place had not been maintained. Joash remained on his guard but it wouldn't take long before he heard Kelsey's voice.

"Joash, we've found her."

Chapter 21: The Coronation

The sky was clear and the sun was shining bright on the city of Horizon. The streets were filled with people making their way towards the castle in an orderly manner. Guards were scattered throughout to ensure the public would follow the rules. All things seemed to be pointing at the perfect day, but in contrast, it couldn't have been further from the truth.

Looking down from her window was Lady Athaliah, who was preparing for her big day. She looked at everything she had plotted for and sacrificed to gain. No price seemed too high as she was about to have everything she ever wanted.

She turned away from the window and sat down on an elegant chair where a few of her servants were tending to her needs. They were making sure her dress was properly fitted. Then they had to ensure her nails and hair were done precisely to her liking. However, her demanding nature grew out of hand as she began scolding her servants.

"Excuse me! What do you think you are doing?!"

"I'm filing your nails, your honour."

"This nail is far too sharp! I could have scarred my face if I tried to scratch myself. And who knows, I could bleed out after that! Is that what you are trying to do?"

"No my lady, I would never..."

"I have heard enough! To exile with you!"

Athaliah silenced her servant, who was forced to leave her presence. Now the other two servants were frozen with fear.

"What are you two doing just standing there?! My hair and nails still need to be fixed!"

Nervously, they approached her and continued working with fear running through their body. Shortly after, someone barged into the room without any permission. It was Haman, and running into the room with him was one of the other servants.

"My apologies your honour. I begged him not to disturb you but he wouldn't listen and..." Before she could continue, Athaliah held out her hand.

"Leave us be."

Everyone except Athaliah and Haman left the room. On their way out, one of the servants closed the door.

"Someone is dressed rather gracefully today. Special occasion?"

"Why are you here?"

"What? I came here to congratulate you on your big day."

"We both know that is a lie. Now tell me why you are here."

"Relax, I'm not here to ruin your big day. I'm here to make sure you remember our deal."

"Just ensure no one disrupts my coronation and you will have your freedom back on the surface."

"Excellent." He began walking away. "Looking forward to your reign."

When he left the room, Athaliah's servants returned. However, the visit from Haman made her more paranoid. She decided to summon one of the commanders into the room.

"You've summoned me?"

"Yes. Commander, I would like you to double the security. We need more along the perimeter of the castle and near the throne where I will be standing."

The commander spoke back in a hesitant tone. "But my lady, our forces are already spread thin. We don't have enough..."

"Excuse me commander, are you saying the safety of your queen is not of the utmost importance?!"

"No your honour, I would never..."

"Good! Then I suggest you figure out a way to solve our current problem."

"The only soldiers we have left are the ones stationed at the border of the city..."

"Excellent, have them moved near where the coronation will take place!"

"But your majesty, what if..."

"You may leave my presence now commander."

The commander stood up and walked away but not without feeling disdain for how he was treated.

Musical instruments were playing and performers were dancing on the castle grounds to keep the people entertained. There were soldiers scattered throughout the castle, some on the lower level, some on the high levels, and some wandering indoors. All to make sure nothing would ruin this momentous day.

The music went on for a little longer before the performers received a signal to slowly stop playing their instruments. The performers halted and moved to the side as a massive horn sounded. A man who was well-dressed with a strong voice stepped up and announced that Lady Athaliah was arriving.

Everyone in the crowd went silent as she sauntered down the red carpet. The audience looked at her with a mix of emotions. Many of them were confused as to whether Athaliah would be a good fit to lead them but out of fear, no one objected.

After walking up to the center of the platform, she was met with a couple of guards, one standing on the right and one to the left of a priest dressed in robes. He was going to conduct the ceremony and when he saw everyone in place, he lifted up his hands, signalling the beginning of the coronation.

He addressed the audience, and after a long-winded speech, he asked Athaliah to step forward and kneel down. As she followed his instructions, a soldier presented the crown that was kept safe in a small chest. The priest meticulously placed the crown onto her head and when it was tightly secured, Athaliah stood up and the priest announced to the crowd their new queen.

A wave of applause could be heard through the audience and although Athaliah was enjoying every moment of it, she had something important she wanted to tell everyone.

"Thank you. I know it's been a difficult struggle as the famine has taken a toll on you and your families. To make matters worse, you were all abandoned and betrayed by your previous queen. I'm here to ensure that we will persevere through this famine and bring justice to the crimes of the previous queen."

She paused to allow a group of soldiers to bring Alex to the center of the stage. She had shackles on her wrist as she stood in front of the large crowd. The soldiers then forced her to kneel down in front of a stone block. While she was on her knees, a man wearing an executioner mask walked onto the stage holding a giant axe.

The crowd was in shock. Although many of them were unhappy with Alex's disappearance, they did not think she deserved the punishment that was given to her. Athaliah sensed that there was a divide in the audience.

"I will now present my solution to curing the famine."

Entering onto the platform was Haman, causing confusion and chatter amongst the crowd.

"What's that man doing there?"

"Isn't he from the underground?"

"Get that filthy undergrounder out of here!"

After hearing all the noises, Haman took center stage.

"Thank you Queen Athaliah for allowing me to grace this stage. As you all know, I'm the commissioner from the underground arena. I hope we can put all that aside as we move forward together to create a city that will no longer be ravaged by this famine. In fact, I have the perfect solution."

The crowd was stunned by the confidence in his statement but someone spoke up. "And what is your idea exactly?"

"Well, the problem really isn't the famine, it's that there are too many mouths to feed. If we reduce that number down, then less people would have to starve."

"HE'S SUGGESTING GENOCIDE!" someone in the crowd yelled.

"Oh that's rather aggressive. Think of it more as a selection process. The strong survive and the weak fall."

As he concluded, some of his forces from the underground appeared before the audience. The crowd, filled with fear, looked to Queen Athaliah to protect them but she remained silent. Realizing that the queen was not going to save them, the people all began to shoving each other aside, only caring about their own safety.

Because of the coronation ceremony, many of the civilians were already gathered in a confined space. They had nowhere to run as Haman's underground fighters drew closer to the citizens. It was easy pickings as they drew their weapons, but before they could take another step, a horn sounded.

Haman's men diverted their attention to where the sound came from. Haman looked to see who sounded the horn and he began to boil in anger. "Caleb!" He then commanded his men, "Get him!"

With the fighters now moving towards Caleb, all the civilians were able to breathe a bit easier. However, there was one person who grew aggravated by the turn of events.

"What are you all doing?! Stop! Don't you all go chasing after one person!" Athaliah yelled in frustration.

However, it was no use. Haman's personal vendetta against Caleb could not be ignored. She watched as all of Haman's fighters left, leaving her alone. For a moment she was vulnerable and taking advantage of this was someone hiding amongst the crowd in a black cloak.

The person swiftly appeared behind Athaliah and before she could process what was happening, the mysterious person held out her blade near Athaliah's face. Seeing their recently appointed queen in trouble, a plethora of soldiers surrounded the area but they were kept at a distance with the threat of the queen's life. Athaliah held out her hands, communicating to the soldiers to stand down.

"Who are you and who do you think you are?"

"Who I am matters not. However, if you value your face, then let the queen go."

"Haha, who are you talking about? I am the queen."

"You are no queen. Now let Queen Alexandra go. Or you are about to have a few new scars on your face."

With her hand, Athaliah motioned it to tell the executioner to step aside. The masked man put his axe away and stepped off the stage, leaving Alex alone. The assailant knew she wouldn't be allowed to escape without taking a hostage, so she tied Athaliah's wrist behind her back and kept her close. They moved towards Alex and the mysterious person spoke with her.

"Can you move?"

"Yes, I can."

"Good, let's get out of here. We'll use this rotten witch as our hostage."

"Wait, whoever you are, you don't have to risk your life to do this." Alex insisted but not wanting to explain further, the mysterious rescuer removed her hood. Athaliah had no idea who it was but Alex could instantly recognize her.

"Windsor! What are you doing here?"

"I'm here to save you mom."

"You don't have to put your life at risk like this... Wait, what did you call me?"

Before Windsor could respond, Athaliah interjected. "No way. I didn't recognize you at first, but now I see it. Windsor, you have grown up so much. It's so good to see you reunited with your mother."

"Be quiet witch." Windsor fought back.

"Windsor? You are... my daughter?"

Chapter 22: Caleb and Haman

Caleb continued running out into the city and turned into an alley. He was followed closely by Haman and his forces, forcing him into a dead end. They had their weapons out, approaching him slowly, thinking they had him cornered. However, Caleb wasn't concerned despite being outnumbered fifteen to one.

They continued advancing, anticipating their revenge but suddenly, they all felt the ground shaking. Initially some of them thought it was an earthquake but Haman could sense it was something else entirely. When he looked to the side, he could see a herd of rams heading their way. Leading the pack was someone riding on the alpha ram, Shepherd.

Haman was able to dive out of the way, but the rest of his minions were swept away by the herd. When the underground commissioner got back on his feet, he was met by his nemesis, Caleb, who stood before him.

When their eyes met, they both drew out their weapons; Caleb with his sword, and Haman pulled out a staff with a viper's head at the top. They charged towards each other and their weapons clashed.

"Well look who decided to return. You really think you can best me in a fight?"

Caleb didn't reply with words. There was little to no expression on his face, which threw Haman off.

"Don't you ignore me when I'm talking to you!" He grew aggravated by Caleb's aloofness and advanced towards his enemy.

Little did Haman know, some of Caleb's memories had returned to him. He knew the truth about his past and who Haman really was. With all this knowledge, he gripped his sword, and met Haman in the middle of the battlefield. The weapons resonated as the two fighters stared at each other down. Their struggle felt familiar and brought out some repressed memories of their past.

Many years ago...

Two boys at the young age of nine years old, each held a wooden sword in their hand. They both let out a loud warcry before dashing towards each other with all their might. Both swung their weapons simultaneously and to their dismay, no victor was declared that day as their battle ended in a draw.

Exhausted, the two boys found a quiet alley in the slums to sit and rest. One of them had two cans of soda and he handed the other one to his friend.

"Haman, you don't have any money, where did you get these?"

"I've got many talents that you don't know about."

"You stole them?!"

"Relax, I actually paid for these ones. I knew you would make a big fuss about it."

"Well, in that case, thanks Haman!" Caleb opened up the can, and once the fizz noise was gone, he took a huge gulp from it.

"Caleb, we got to get out of this place."

"And go where?"

"To the city, where the streets are clean and where people will no longer look down on us because we live in the slums."

"That's going to be tough. No one has ever made it out of the slums and into the city without being arrested by those guards."

"Tch, is the great Caleb scared?"

"Ha, hardly. That just means we are going to be the first to do it!"

"I would expect nothing less. Let's work together and make it happen."

The two boys shook each other's hand to signify their unified goal. Together they were going to find a way to escape the slums and live in the city where they thought they would find freedom.

Ten years later...

As they grew up, Haman and Caleb attempted to leave the slums, but they would always be seen by the soldiers of Horizon. Luckily, they were extremely nimble and agile, which allowed them to escape every time.

However, with each passing day, Haman's disdain for the people of the city grew. He couldn't stand how some people got to live a lavish lifestyle based on where they were born, while the less fortunate had to suffer. Because of this, Haman began going to the city to steal from the local businesses.

Caleb knew that what Haman was doing was wrong, but being loyal to his friend, he couldn't abandon him. He stayed close to him on all his heists to make sure Haman would never step over the line. However, on one trip, they were spotted by a soldier on patrol. Caleb and Haman managed to subdue the soldier, who lay on the ground unconscious.

Caleb was going to leave the man alone as if nothing happened, but Haman's anger took over him. With his weapon in hand, he was ready to end the life of the unresponsive soldier but Caleb stepped in.

"That's enough, let's get out of here."

But Haman would not listen. He was prepared to strike down the defenseless man but Caleb tackled him to the ground.

"Caleb! What are you doing? Why are you saving the enemy?"

"No, I'm not on their side. But I am stopping you from making an irreversible mistake."

"Tch, you are a traitor!"

"No, Haman I'm trying to help..."

He was cut off as a group of armoured soldiers barged into the store. Caleb and Haman had a temporary ceasefire and began fighting the enemies before them. Although they were experienced fighters, there were too many soldiers to take on in such a confined space. Realizing their *chances of winning were low, Caleb saw the backdoor and told Haman to retreat. Unfortunately, Haman couldn't hear his words as he continued to aggressively fight the soldiers.*

Knowing his friend would have been overwhelmed and arrested, Caleb jumped back into the fray to help Haman. Although Caleb helped him take out a couple of the soldiers, Haman was furious as his pride got the better of him. However, Caleb pushed Haman out of the way, towards the back exit.

As Haman was picking himself up, he saw reinforcements approaching. Caleb fought back but in doing so, he received a scar on his face and was apprehended. Haman realized his mistake and wanted to help Caleb but it was too late. Caleb told Haman to run, because if he didn't escape now, they would both be detained. So he left through the backdoor and escaped from the soldiers, but he would never forget how his friend risked his life so he could have another chance. From that day, Haman's hate for the city grew to new heights and he wanted nothing more than to get his revenge.

So Haman began recruiting the toughest fighters he could find in the slums. To ensure they were strong enough to take down the soldiers, he created the underground fights. The contest was meant to weed out the weak, finding only the strongest that could take on the soldiers of the city and save his friend from prison.

When he finally had his forces assembled, he made his return to the city of Horizon where he was met with Queen Alexandra and her royal guards. Haman demanded that they release Caleb from his prison but to his dismay, one of the soldiers removed their helm, revealing his face. Haman couldn't believe his eyes, but Caleb had become one of the royal soldiers of Horizon.

Haman was so shocked to see Caleb in alliance with the enemy. He turned and retreated with his minions, even though Caleb shouted out in an attempt to speak with him. But he ignored it, thinking his once close friend had been possessed or mind controlled. As he was leaving the city feeling defeated, he was met with a woman who had her identity concealed, blocking their path.

"I don't know who you think you are, but I suggest you move out of my way."

The woman in the cloak did not move. Haman commanded his men to attack her simultaneously but suddenly, a menacing shadow appeared before them. No one ever got a chance to even catch a glimpse of what the creature looked like as it instantly wiped out Haman's forces in seconds.

After their defeat, the shadow returned to the cloak woman who slowly approached Haman. He wasn't running away, but his heart was pounding after what he had witnessed.

"Relax, despite how you have greeted me, my intentions for meeting you have not changed."

"What do you want?"

"Oh, this isn't about what I want. It's about how I can help you get what you want."

"What are you talking about?"

"I know who you are. Haman of the slums, who has a deep hatred for the people of Horizon. Oh, and you also lost your best friend to that mind controlling witch, Queen Alexandra."

"So what?"

"I can help you get your friend back and get revenge on both the queen and the people of the city." Haman's interest was piqued. "Just swear your allegiance to me and you will have what you want." She held out her hand and although he hesitated for a moment, he ended up grabbing hold of her hand. At that very moment, the pact was sealed.

"From that day on, I did everything she asked. I kidnapped Windsor first and then Shepherd was next. However, Council member Kelsey caught wind of our plan. Because of her, one of your soldiers, Joash, along with a mysterious man I didn't recognize, took Shepherd away.

You stayed behind to stall for them but eventually you were overwhelmed and captured. Athaliah was going to lock you away and torture you but I asked her to release you into my custody.

She handed you over to me but not before wiping away your memories of the city. Knowing this, I did everything in my power to ensure you would not encounter Athaliah, Queen Alexandra, and your children.

"That's why you kept me in the underground arena!"

He nodded. "I knew you would do everything in your power to remain as the champion of the underground arena. That way you would stay and never remember the past, stopping you from getting into any danger in the city."

Caleb was having mixed emotions. He realized his former friend was trying to keep him safe. In contrast, he felt angry that he had been lied to for so long. He wanted to confront Haman further but suddenly, his friend's strength drastically decreased. Caleb rushed to his side.

"Haman!"

"I'm sorry, for what I have done..."

"You can still turn things around."

"No Caleb, I'm sorry. But I sold my soul away. Forgive me."

A dark circle appeared around Haman. Caleb stayed and attempted to save his former friend but Haman pushed him away. Caleb got back up and was ready to run back but Haman held his hand out to signal his old friend to stop. In his final moment, he weakly uttered a few words to Caleb.

"She has your third..."

However, before he could finish, a giant dark hand appeared beneath Haman and grabbed him. His soul was dragged down into the abyss where it would be sacrificed. Caleb looked in horror as he had lost his childhood friend.

Chapter 23: Family Reunion

When Windsor's blade was inches away from Athaliah's face, her weapon stopped in its place. A dark shadow appeared behind Athaliah, preventing Windsor from striking her. Despite that, Windsor forced her sword onto her enemy but the shadow's aura repelled Windsor away, sending her to the ground.

As she tried to get up, Windsor found herself surrounded by the dark shadow that shrouded Athaliah. The darkness began to engulf her body and the mask reappeared on her face.

When Alex saw what happened, she was concerned for her daughter. She ran to her daughter, but Windsor swung her blade which barely missed her mother. Alex found herself with her back on the ground and as she pulled herself up, she was met with a blade pointing right at her face.

"What did you do to her?" Alex directed her anger towards Athaliah, who stood with a devious smile.

"Oh I didn't do anything, but I might know why she's acting this way."

"What do you mean? You brainwashed her!"

"Tch, I did no such thing. However, you did something that she won't forget."

"What?"

"You abandoned her in her time of greatest need. She was all alone, lost in the dark, while you were tending to your duties as queen."

"No, I didn't know. You altered my memories and..."

"Excuses!" Atahliah walked to Windsor and spoke close to her ears. "She even left the castle to find your brother, but not for you!"

Windsor reacted by kicking Alex with great force. She was sent back a couple meters as she held her abdomen. Windsor slowly walked towards her mother with her blade in hand. Alex got to one knee and used all her effort to try and communicate with her.

"Windsor, I..." She only got out those words before getting kicked again. Then she was picked up and thrown away. With Windsor approaching again and her blade raised in the air, Alex spoke again, trying to reach her.

"It's no use, she can't hear your voice."

Athaliah watched with a wicked smile as the queen's demise seemed imminent. She saw the blade swinging downward and was anticipating a glorious celebration but instead, she was met with disappointment.

Although there was a cut on Alex's arm, the wound was minor compared to what Athaliah was expecting. What she saw was Windsor embraced by her mother despite her hostile intent. Windsor's arms were shaking, fighting against her possessed body to protect her mother.

"Why are you hesitating? She abandoned you and left you all alone. End her!"

Her body continued to shake as Windsor struggled to regain control.

"It's okay Windsor. I'm here for you. This time, I'm not going anywhere."

Athaliah could see that the possession magic was beginning to break. Not wanting to further risk her victory, she took control of the situation by invoking her magic. Dark chains appeared, binding around the two women. Alex tried to reach out her hand to her daughter but Athaliah instantly pulled the two apart.

Athaliah first turned to Windsor. "Weak and pathetic. Couldn't even carry out one simple command. I no longer have any use for you." She was about to close her grip, but she was interrupted by Alex.

"Sigh, what do you want?"

"My daughter is far stronger than you will ever be."

"Oh? Is that so?"

"Let her go and find out yourself."

Athaliah paused for a moment, then she suddenly tightened the chains around Alex. She began to yell as the pain intensified.

"Fool, did you really think that would work? For thinking I would fall for such a simple trick, I will deal with you first."

As Athaliah was about to unleash the full extent of her power on Alex but she was struck from her blindside and was knocked down. Meanwhile, Alex got a moment to catch her breath and she got to see who had arrived to save her.

"Shepherd!"

"So, the prodigal son has finally decided to show his face."

Shepherd ignored Athaliah and went straight to his mother. He kneeled down as she was lying on the ground. Alex placed her hand on his face to ensure she wasn't hallucinating.

"It's really you!"

"Yeah mom, I'm back."

"You have grown so much..."

Their moment was interrupted as Athaliah refused to be ignored.

"Hey! How dare you ignore me. Do you know who I am? I'm the Queen of..."

She stopped mid-sentence as a knife flew past her face. For a moment, she stood frozen, then she moved her right hand towards her cheek. With her two fingers, she gently wiped her cheek, where she felt a cut followed by some blood.

"You insolent child!" She raised her hand, ready to cast her dark magic.

Seeing this, Shepherd moved away from Alex so she wouldn't get caught in the crossfire. Athaliah aimed and unleashed a dark bolt at her target. "You will bow to me." She followed up with a barrage of dark blasts. "And beg for mercy!" Each attack caused an explosion and created a huge smoke cloud.

Queen Athaliah was speechless when the smoke cleared. Out of the dust stood Shepherd who was unscathed. He began walking towards Athliah, who spoke with fear in her voice.

"What? Impossible!" As Shepherd continued walking towards her, she kept casting her magic against him. With the blast approaching, he slightly moved his head to avoid the attacks. In addition to each miss, Athaliah's fear grew.

"How? How is this possible?!" He was now in front of her striking her in the gut. She attempted to counter by swiping her nails at Shepherd but he was too nimble. He evaded her hand and then retaliated by grabbing her arm and throwing her against the ground.

"You are just a lowly shepherd boy. How could you be doing this to me?!" She voiced her frustration as she slowly got up.

"It's true, I am a shepherd boy, which means not only have I learned how to fight for myself but also to protect those I care about." He paused and then gave her a stern look. "You, on the other hand, have lived your life through your lies and deceit. You have no idea how to truly fight, and that is why you are weak."

Athaliah was baffled by what Shepherd had said. She lowered her head, giving off the impression that she had been defeated, but suddenly, she let out a sinister laugh. Shepherd thought she had lost her mind but Alex had a terrible feeling.

"Hahahaha, you? Talking to me like that? You are a murderer."

"Murderer? What is she talking about?" Alex said while looking at her son.

"Oh? You mean you don't know? Well, let me enlighten you. The one who murdered the soldier in the town of Mahlon, was HIM!" Athaliah pointed at Shepherd.

"That can't be true. Shepherd!" She turned to face her son who couldn't meet her eyes.

"I..." He couldn't find the words either. It was at this moment that Shepherd became vulnerable and Athaliah could sense it. She took advantage of the opportunity by recasting her dark chains. In seconds, she had both Shepherd and Alex all wrapped up.

"Fools. You really thought you could defeat me? She had decided Shepherd would be her first victim, but she also made sure Alex and Windsor could see what she was about to do.

"Stop! What are you doing?!" Alex cried out.

"Your son committed the crime of murder. This is retribution for what he has done." She said with the most sinister smile.

Windsor was struggling to break free but with her mask still on, she still wasn't fully herself. Athaliah noticed and immediately made a fist directed at Windsor. Suddenly, Windsor felt a massive shock through her entire body and she shook uncontrollably.

"Stop this! It's me you want, let them go!" Alex pleaded but Athaliah ignored her cries. She was enjoying every moment of what was happening.

"Now, you know what it feels like to have everything taken from you."

"Why are you doing all this?!" Alex asked in desperation.

Athaliah stopped for a moment. A rush of thoughts ran through her mind about what happened in her past. It was something she could never let go of. More importantly, it was the reason why she made it this far.

Years ago, the city of Horizon was a prosperous city filled with food and riches throughout the land. There was no segregation as everyone lived united under the protection of the royal family. Everyone enjoyed their lives as there was little to no major conflict.

One such family who enjoyed the benefits of such an amazing city was none other than Athaliah's. She was happily married with three children, all of whom she raised. Life was good and Athaliah was anticipating to see her children grow up to become successful adults. Unfortunately, that would never happen.

A plague fell upon the city, claiming many lives. It forced a major part of the population to be segregated into what was now known as the slums. In the midst of the calamity, all her children grew extremely sick. She tried saving them, but the soldiers from the castle appeared and their orders were to keep the people of the slums contained to prevent the plague from spreading.

Having already lost two of her children to the plague, Athaliah begged them to take her remaining child and get him treatment but the soldiers refused. Because of this, she lost her final child and blamed the royal family for everything she had lost.

After the plague subsided, Athaliah worked her way out of the slums and into the city palace. Her influence grew so much that she became a council member, right when Alexandra was about to be crowned the queen. Immediately, Athaliah pinpointed the person who would be the target for her vengeance.

Alexandra finally understood the motive behind Athaliah's actions. She wanted to speak with Athaliah, but the angry sorceress would have none of it.

"Silence!" She unleashed a force that sent Alex slamming onto the ground. "Your empty words mean nothing." She tightened the chains that were on Shepherd and he began suffocating.

"Now, you will know my pain. First, starting with your son!"

Alex screamed as Athaliah was about to cast the final spell but at the last moment, she sensed something being thrown her way. It was a sword that missed her face but slashed off a bit of her hair. She looked at the person who dared trifle against her and it was none other than Caleb.

He pulled Shepherd away from her and he slowly walked towards where Alex was lying.

"Well, you have definitely seen better days." Caleb fired at her.

"And you sure took your sweet time."

They would have continued their banter but Caleb noticed Windsor had the mask attached to her face.

"I'm guessing that witch is responsible for this." Alex nodded. Caleb then gently placed Shepherd down before standing back up.

"Watch over them. I won't be long."

"Tch, the outcast warrior makes his return."

Caleb wasted no time as he swiftly attacked Athaliah. In an instant, she was on her knees with a sword pierced through the right side of her body.

"Im... Impossible! With all that power in the palm of my hands. How could you... Hey, don't you dare turn your back and walk away from me!"

"I don't speak to weaklings like you."

"What did you call me? How dare you say that to me!"

"Whatever, you already lost." Caleb continued walking in the opposite direction.

"No, I haven't! Come back here and fight me!"

Caleb ignored her and made his way to Shepherd. He tapped him on the shoulder and Shepherd slowly began to open his eyes.

"Finally decided to wake up?"

Shepherd had a tear run down his face as he jumped into his father's arms.

"I'm sorry dad."

"Huh? What for?"

"I couldn't defeat Athaliah by myself. You must be really disappointed."

"Shepherd, you survived many years without my guidance and you protected both your mother and sister. I couldn't be more proud."

"You mean it?"

"Absolutely!"

After a peaceful moment, Caleb noticed Alex nearby trying to get his attention. She was concerned about something but wasn't sure what it was until he looked over to Windsor. She was lying on the ground and the mask was still stuck to her face. Immediately, Caleb reacted by turning to Athaliah in a furious rage.

"Take that mask off my daughter now!"

"Tch, as if I would take orders from you." The witch refused. "Besides, she's not the one you need to be worried about."

Caleb froze for a moment, confused as he looked at Alex and Shepherd.

"What is she talking about?" Alex asked Caleb.

Caleb immediately looked at Athaliah and threatened her. "Don't you dare drag her into this..."

"Who are you talking about? You're going to have to be more clear!" Athaliah taunted him.

"Freyja, our third child!"

Suddenly, a rush of memories came back to Alex and her demeanor changed. "Where is she? Give her back you monster!"

"Hahaha! You have nothing to threaten me with."

Caleb and Alex felt defeated as they struggled to find a solution to their dilemma.

"Awe, don't look so grim as if all hope is lost. In fact, I'm feeling quite generous right now. IF you do everything I demand, then I will consider letting your precious little Freyja live."

"You're lying. How do we even know you have my sister?" Shepherd jumped in.

"You don't. But are you really going to take that chance?"

Caleb and Alex glanced at each other as they put their hands up to surrender.

"Mom! Dad! Stop, it's a trap!"

"Shepherd, everything is going to be alright." Caleb tried to assure him.

"No! Don't do it!"

"Shepherd." Alex chimed in. "Take care of your sister for us."

Shepherd mustered what strength he had left and ran towards them, at the same time, Athaliah casted a dark pulse that aimed straight for his parents. He would only watch as the blast was about to strike two of the most important people in his life. However, before the pulse made contact, someone jumped in between and took the hit.

"Uncle Joash!" Shepherd called out in shock.

"Great to see you kid." His uncle greeted.

"But how? I thought you were..." Shepherd stopped as he noticed his uncle was about to fall, so he caught him.

"Thanks, I'll be okay."

"Tch, another nuisance, but this changes nothing!" Athaliah claimed.

"Actually, you should take a closer look." Joash pointed out.

Bewildered, Athaliah scanned the vicinity until her eyes met with an intimidating figure. It was council member Kelsey and she was holding someone in her arms.

"Freyja!" Alex immediately recognized her daughter when Kelsey brought her over.

"No! Impossible! How did you know?!?!" Athaliah yelled in outrage.

"You told me. Don't you remember?" Kelsey responded with a smile.

Although flustered, Athaliah had a flashback of when she was torturing Kelsey in the dungeon. Athaliah realizes she mentioned where she was keeping Freyja. Now with Freyja free, she had no leverage. Caleb stood with anger in his eyes. In contrast, Athaliah was shaking and filled with fear.

Athaliah mindlessly unleashed a barrage of dark magical blasts striking Caleb who remained still. Everyone was holding their breath while Athaliah was laughing maniacally.

"Hahaha, that's right! I can't lose! No one can stop..."

The smoke began to clear and Caleb was standing. Despite some bruises and a destroyed chestplate, he seemed unfazed and more importantly, the tattoos on his arm began to glow. The sheep, the fire, and the wind were all radiating, giving him strength.

Athaliah grew furious and channeled all her energy into one concentrated attack. As the blast headed towards Caleb, he met it head on and sliced through the attack with his sword. Almost immediately after that, he appeared on the other side of Athaliah. Everything seemed to have stood still for a moment and then, Athaliah collapsed.

For a moment, Athaliah could see her children. They seemed to be within reach, so she raised her hand in hopes to hold them but suddenly, the world went dark and everything shattered. Her greed for vengeance had taken over her heart completely. She laid on the ground, alone.

With Athaliah's defeat, the glow in Caleb's tattoos vanished. Exhausted, he was dropping to his knees but he was caught in Shepherd's embrace. He looked at his son and Shepherd guided his father's gaze to Windsor without the possessed mask on her face.

"You two doing alright?" He asked despite feeling pain throughout his body.

"Yeah, thanks to you dad." Shepherd said with a proud voice.

"That's good..." he was cut off as Windsor gave him a big hug.

"Don't scare us like that again!"

"Alright, I'll do my best."

Alex then appeared with Freyja in her arms. "Well, you did it. I don't know how, but you somehow brought us all back together."

"I guess I did pretty good."

"You did alright." They both laughed as Shepherd and Windsor looked at each other puzzled.

"Okay you two lovebirds, let's get out of here." Windsor nagged them.

"Yeah I'm pretty hungry." Shepherd added.

"Uh hello, we are still in the middle of a famine..."

"That's why I'm hungry!"

"Alright you two. Help me up and we'll figure out..."

Suddenly, there was a sense of dread that filled the atmosphere. They turned their attention to where Athaliah's body was, and an ominous energy shrouded her body. A dark magical circle appeared beneath her as her body was offered as a sacrifice. In her place, appeared a malignant creature. It had the anatomy of a human but it had horns on its head, glowing red eyes and spikes on the joints of its body.

It stood up, stretching and cracking its joints. When it was done warming up, it fixed its eyes on the family. They could feel a terrifying aura about the creature but they stood firm together.

"You must be the ones responsible for defeating that witch."

Caleb nodded nervously but he remained vigilant of the creature's movement.

"Well then, I would like to thank you all. It was a nightmare beginning trapped in that accursed body. As a token of my appreciation I will spare your lives.

"Who are you?" Asked Caleb.

"Oh my apologies. I'm Greed, one of the greatest sins of mankind."

"What are you going to do to everyone else?" Alex asked in a worried tone.

"Allow me to demonstrate."

He held out his hand and snapped his fingers. Within seconds, the sky began to darkened and a veil encased the entire city. Caleb, Alex, Windsor, Shepherd, Freyja, Joash, and Kelsey were unaffected but the same could not be said for everyone else.

A sudden burst of anger could be heard throughout the castle as the civilians and soldiers went into hysteria. Everyone began fighting amongst each other senselessly with no restraint.

"What did you do to them?!" Shepherd questioned.

"I didn't do anything to them. All I did was allow them to express their most inner desires, GREED!"

"This isn't greed. This is senseless violence!" Windsor argued.

"Oh? You are one to talk, my little Windsor. Remember the loneliness you felt after being abandoned? Your greed for attention allowed you to be controlled by me." Windsor held her head as she felt a massive headache.

"That's enough! You leave my daughter out of this!" Caleb shouted in anger.

"Relax, I have no use for your daughter any longer. Just look around you."

They didn't have to search far to see some of the soldiers and people fighting aggressively against each other.

"Everything one does stems from greed."

He pointed to the crowd of people fighting for food, money, and valuables. "The greed for possessions."

He then moved to Caleb. "Greed for pride and fame." That was when Caleb remembered about his time in the underground fights.

Then he went to Shepherd. "Greed for vengeance." Shepherd remembered being so blinded by his rage, thinking he had lost Uncle Joash.

Lastly, he moved towards Alex. "Greed for knowledge." Alex remembered when she first heard about Caleb and Shepherd. She abandoned her people wanting to know where her family was.

"Everyone is susceptible to greed!"

After hearing that, Shepherd and Caleb drew their weapons in hopes to strike him but with only his bare hands, he halted their attack. Despite the father-son duo working together, they couldn't leave a scratch on Greed. He then increased his strength and the sheer force of his aura repelled them back, slamming them at opposite ends of the battlefield.

Greed decided to attack Shepherd who managed to pick up his staff to parry Greed's assault. Shepherd struggled to hold his ground and he could feel that he was being pushed back. However, Windsor had snapped out of her confused state and saw the opening that her brother had created for her. Unfortunately, Greed had sensed her presence long before she got near. Without looking, he grabbed her face and dropped her against the ground.

"Windsor!" Shepherd was enraged as he attempted to get revenge for his sister. Greed wasn't fazed, as he picked up Windsor and threw her against her brother.

Caleb was now slowly getting up on his feet. When he finally shook off the last hit, he saw the horror that was unfolding before his eyes. Greed had his hand over his son and daughter. With rage overtaking his body, he recklessly charged towards his enemy but Greed grabbed him in midair. With a furious swing, Greed slammed Caleb to the ground, leaving the brave warrior unconscious.

Greed stood alone and looked around at his victory. The two siblings, Windsor and Shepherd were lying close to one another with wounds throughout their body. A few meters away from them was their dad, Caleb, who also had his eyes closed and unable to move. No one was left to stop Greed as he was ready to siphon their souls, starting with Windsor's.

Chapter 24: Greed

Shepherd woke up in his mind where he was surrounded by a mysterious mist.

"Hey! Is anybody there? Windsor? Mom? Dad? Uncle Joash?"

When it was clear nobody was around, he sat down holding his hands over his head. Slowly, he remembered the events that took place before he found himself here. His family was in danger but there was nothing he could do. He continued to lament until he noticed footsteps that had appeared near him. Initially, he was excited to find out he wasn't alone until he saw the man's face. It was the same person he bumped into on the farm and the mysterious tomb.

"Are you here to make jokes and rub my failures in my face?"

"Make fun of you? Most likely, but what's this about your failures?"

"My family is in danger and it's because of me."

"Oh and what makes you say that?"

"Out of everyone in my family, I'm irrelevant. Windsor is skilled with the sword, my mom is incredibly wise, and my dad is an amazing fighter. But me, I got nothing."

There was a moment of silence that Shepherd was not expecting. He looked up to find the man hadn't walked too far from him.

"Your name, tell me, who gave it to you?"

"My parents."

"And why did they give you that name?"

"Because I..." He stopped.

"Just reflect."

Memories of when Shepherd would protect his sheep from wolves popped up in his mind. There was also a time when he and his sister were lost in the forest and Windsor was injured. Shepherd kept her safe from a terrifying bear. Although he didn't defeat the predator on his own, he stalled long enough for his father to arrive and defeat the bear.

"It's not just your name that creates your identity but your experiences as well."

Hearing this, Shepherd's spirit was reinvigorated, but a memory of greed for vengeance was hindering him. "Ahh! But there is darkness in my heart. How could I..."

"Everyone struggles with something, but regardless, some push forward despite their deficiencies."

Shepherd was able to stare down the vengeful spirit and slowly, his spirit overcame and dissipated the darkness. He was about to thank the man but he could hear his sister in danger.

"Windsor! I got to go, thank you for..."

When he turned around, the man was gone. Although he was left with many questions, he rushed to follow his sister's voice.

Windsor was wandering in an empty void filled with darkness. She called out to Caleb, Alex and Shepherd. Within seconds, she saw a silhouette of her family in the distance. With haste, she ran to embrace them but once she got near, the silhouette faded away.

"Oh so close, yet so far!" A voice similar to Windsor's could be heard, only it sounded more sinister.

"Who are you?" She frantically looked around.

Suddenly, emerging from the shadows beneath the ground was a dark clone of Windsor with a possessed mask over her face. "I'm you!"

The clone swiftly swung her blade which Windsor reacted in time to deflect but she was still knocked off balance.

She attempted to get up but the clone was relentless. It ruthlessly continued to attack Windsor who was barely keeping up. Eventually, her weapon was knocked out of her hands. The clone's weapon was now held at Windsor's neck.

"Look at you. Weak! You are nothing without me!"

While Windsor was emotionally vulnerable, she began hearing cries for help. She saw a vision of Caleb and Shepherd unconscious while Alex and Freyja's lives were being threatened.

"You aren't strong enough to save them. But I can." The doppelganger let out her hand for Windsor to accept.

Windsor was caught in a dilemma. If she accepted the offer, she would never be herself again. Despite that, she cared about her family more. She slowly reached out her hand to her shadowy duplicate. They were close to sealing the deal, however, Shepherd's spirit intervened.

"Shepherd! What are you... How are you even here?!"

"I don't know either but who cares about that. Whatever you do, don't..."

Shepherd never finished his words. Instead, Windsor witnessed a shadowy blade pierce through her brother's heart. Without a chance to say another word, he fainted on the spot. Windsor was disheartened by the sight as she was frozen on her knees.

"Don't worry about him. There is no way he could be your brother. He is far too weak. Now, accept my offer and we will save your family together!"

This time, the clone didn't even wait for Windsor's response. It reached out its hand and was ready to grab Windsor's. It was inches away from grasping what it wanted but Windsor swatted the hand away.

The shadow clone was startled but to compound her problems, it could sense Windsor's aura had completely changed.

"Don't you dare insult my brother!"

The doppelganger was now shaking, and in its fear, it attempted to strike without thinking. However, Windsor's fighting instinct had been restored. With one swing, the shadows began to disperse and her soul was finally free.

Caleb woke up to the sound of cheering. He looked around to see the large crowd in the stance cheering his name. He was confused as to what was happening until he looked back to where he stood. He saw many fighters lying on the ground defeated. Before he could fully process what had happened, he heard a loud voice speaking to the crowd.

"Ladies and gentlemen! Give it up for the champion of the battle royale, CALEB!"

"Caleb! Caleb! Caleb!" The crowd continued to chant his name.

He was enjoying the moment when suddenly, the entire place went dark. Caleb now had his guard up, as he heard a different voice.

"Do you miss it?" It was Greed's voice but Caleb tried to ignore him.

"Oh, don't try to hide it. It's very obvious you still want this, and guess what? It can all be yours again."

Caleb opened his eyes.

"Go on. Take it! It's all yours." Greed tempted.

He reached his hand out, about to accept Greed's offer until he saw the tattoos on his arm. At that moment, he was reminded of his family: Alex, Freyja, Windsor and Shepherd. His hand stopped, which surprised Greed.

"Thanks for your generosity, but you can take everything back and shove it up your..."

Before he could finish, Greed struck him in the gut unexpectedly, dropping Caleb to his knees.

"You are a fool to deny my offer. Now you will suffer!"

Caleb was about to accept his fate, when suddenly he had the image of Alex holding Freyja in his mind. He could sense they were in danger, which got him to move. However, Greed was still about to consume his soul.

Caleb would have been done for, but both Windsor and Shepherd's spirit appeared, helping him fight back against Greed's spirit. He was happy to see his two kids working together, as they repelled out the darkness from his mind.

"When did you two learn to get along?" Caleb asked.

"Well, we learned it from you and mom..." Immediately Windsor smacked Shepherd on the back of the head.

"This never happened, so you better not tell mom about any of this." She directed her comment to both of them.

"Haha alright, my lips are sealed. Now, let's go save your sister and mother."

Chapter 25: Reunited

Greed was standing near Windsor and Shepherd's unconscious bodies. He was ready to siphon their souls but appearing in his way was Alex. She bravely stood to protect her children while holding Freyja tightly in her arms.

"The Queen who abandoned her people in their time of need? You don't scare me. Now step aside."

"No. This time, I will not run away."

"Foolish. But admirable. Regardless, your fate will end the same as everyone else!"

He stuck his hand out to siphon their souls. Alex stood her ground and shielded Freyja, expecting the worst.

"What?" Greed was baffled as they remained unharmed. He couldn't drain their souls, so he resorted to striking them instead. He swung his right fist, but a staff intercepted his attack.

"Shepherd!" Alex shouted.

"Don't worry mom, I will protect you and Freyja!"

"Laughable, because you can't even protect yourself!" Greed swung his other hand but this time, a sword parried against it.

"Windsor!"

"I'm here mom and I'll keep an eye on Shepherd for you."

"Hey! I'm a grown man now! I don't need your supervision!"

"Actually, you are still a teenager. Plus, I'm still your older sister."

Even though they were arguing, Alex was happy and proud to see them fighting together.

"Enough! I will destroy you all!"

Greed drew on the power of the souls he siphoned. He was beginning to push back Shepherd and Windsor but then Caleb appeared behind them.

"Dad!" They shouted simultaneously.

With their combined effort, they were about to push Greed back despite his power boost. His frustration was now at its peak and he unleashed a massive energy outburst. He was hoping to finish them off with his next assault. However, he wasn't prepared for what was about to happen next.

"You two ready?" Caleb asked both Windsor and Shepherd.

"Let's get him!" They both affirmed.

As the three stormed forward together, a radiant light appeared before them. In unison they clashed against their powerful enemy and appeared on the opposite side of the battlefield. The light from the three warriors faded and they all began to stumble to the ground. However, they held each other up, preventing them from falling unconscious.

"Ha, all futile. I'm Greed, you can't defeat..."

Shepherd had struck Greed in the knee causing the fiend to stumble. Greed then tried to get up but he felt a massive surge of pain from his upper torso. He looked and saw two giant cuts: one vertical, done by Windsor, and the other horizontal, caused by Caleb.

"Tch, I was actually wounded by you weaklings? No matter, I will have the final laugh."

He still had enough energy to strike down the injured warriors but Alex stood with Freyja in her arms. Despite her interference, Greed fired a dark blast that was about to consume them all. However, someone appeared and blocked the attack. It was the executioner, but his hood had fallen off after deflecting the attack. His face was revealed and it was the mysterious man from the mountain.

"You... What are you doing here?"

"I'm here to let you know your time here is coming to an end."

"Ha, as long as there are humans in this world, I will always exist. For humans will always have greed in their hearts."

"Then I think you better look again." He pointed at Greed and he looked at himself to find that his powers had decreased tremendously.

"What? How...?"

Greed looked at Alex, Caleb, Freyja, Shepherd, and Windsor. They all stood together side by side with all their wounds. Because they were fighting to protect each other, greed could not be found in their hearts.

"Heh, what do you know? You humans got lucky this time. But I will return. For there wil be other humans who will fall to the temptation of greed."

"Don't come back anytime soon." Caleb said.

"Because if you do..." Alex paused.

"We will be there..." Windsor followed.

"To stop you again." Shepherd finished.

He gave a malicious laugh before disappearing into a dark portal. Once the portal vanished as well, Windsor let out a huge sigh of relief as she dropped to the ground.

"Is it finally over?"

Alex looked at Freyja in her arms. Her baby girl was calm and fast asleep with no worry in the world. "Yes, I believe it is. You did well, Windsor." Alex smiled at her daughter.

"All in a day's work. Let's quickly get going because I need a shower pronto!" Caleb was getting ready to leave, but Shepherd still had some unfinished business.

"Wait, there's one more thing we need to do." He turned to face the mysterious man.

"Uh oh. I hope you aren't planning to take your frustration out on me."

"No, I'm here to thank you, for everything."

When Shepherd said those words, Caleb, Alex, and Windsor caught up to him. They were confused as to why their son was thanking the mysterious man.

"Mom, Dad, this is the man who helped save Uncle Joash. He is also a big reason why our family has been reunited today."

The man was walking away but Alex spoke up. "Hey wait. I'm still not sure who you are, but is there anything we can do to repay you?"

"I take no credit. I'm just a messenger sent to do what I'm asked by the One who is great."

"Well that's awfully, cryptic. You got a name or something?" Windsor asked.

"Just call me Rice. That will be good."

"There has to be something we can do to repay you. Come on, just say it!" Caleb kept pressing.

"As long as you love each other as a family and never let greed dominate your heart, that will suffice."

He faced the sun and suddenly, wings appeared on his back. Caleb, Alex, Shepherd, and Windsor all had the look of shock on their faces. Slowly, the man took to the skies and flew into the horizon. It took them a while but they realized that the man was an angel.

"So, what do we do now?" Shepherd asked.

"Well first off, we got to change Freyja. I think she had an accident after all that excitement." Alex said.

"I can help with that!" Caleb volunteered.

"Uhhh, dad. Why don't you let me help mom with that." Windsor interrupted.

"Hey what?! I can totally be useful and help!"

"Caleb, I think Windsor has a point."

"See Dad. Not my words, but mom's"

While all this was happening, Shepherd was just taking it in. He was so happy to be reunited with his family, and he couldn't wait to catch up on all the time they had missed.